He'd come for her.

The wild, reckless boy of her dreams had turned into the dark, dangerous man of her nightmares.

Only his eyes were as she remembered—bold, piercing and purposeful.

He knew.

"You look good. Just as I remembered you," he said.

And he still had the ability to paralyze her—that stomach-quivering, breath-hitching, knee-jellying, mind-numbing power to immobilize her with one curve of his mouth.

He had no right to sashay into her store, into her life. Not after all this time.

"Why don't you crawl out the way you came in?"

Connor's nostrils flared slightly, and the corner of his mouth twitched.

"Same old sassy mouth, too."

Dear Reader,

This May, we celebrate Mother's Day and a fabulous month of uplifting romances. I'm delighted to introduce RITA® Award finalist Carol Stephenson, who debuts with her heartwarming reunion romance, *Nora's Pride*. Carol writes, "*Nora's Pride* is very meaningful to me, as my mother, my staunchest fan and supporter, passed away in May 2000. I'm sure she's smiling down at me from heaven. She passionately believed this would be my first sale." A must-read for your list!

The Princess and the Duke, by Allison Leigh, is the second book in the CROWN AND GLORY series. Here, a princess and a duke share a kiss, but can their love withstand the truth about a royal assassination? We have another heart-thumper from the incomparable Marie Ferrarella with *Lily and the Lawman*, a darling city-girl-meets-small-town-boy romance.

In *A Baby for Emily*, Ginna Gray delivers an emotionally charged love story in which a brooding hero lays claim to a penniless widow who, unbeknownst to her, is carrying *their* child.... Sharon De Vita pulls on the heartstrings with *A Family To Come Home To*, in which a rugged rancher searches for his family and finds true love! You also won't want to miss Patricia McLinn's *The Runaway Bride*, a humorous tale of a sexy cowboy who rescues a distressed bride.

I hope you enjoy these exciting books from Silhouette Special Edition—the place for love, life and family. Come back for more winning reading next month!

Sincerely,

Karen Taylor Richman
Senior Editor

Please address questions and book requests to:
Silhouette Reader Service
U.S.: 3010 Walden Ave., P.O. Box 1325, Buffalo, NY 14269
Canadian: P.O. Box 609, Fort Erie, Ont. L2A 5X3

Nora's Pride

CAROL STEPHENSON

Silhouette

SPECIAL EDITION™

Published by Silhouette Books

America's Publisher of Contemporary Romance

To Mom, with the angels in heaven, and Dad.
Because of your endless love and belief in me,
I reached for the stars and achieved my dreams.
This one is for you with all my love.

 SILHOUETTE BOOKS

ISBN 0-373-24470-3

NORA'S PRIDE

Copyright © 2002 by Carol Stephenson

Printed in U.S.A.

CAROL STEPHENSON

credits her mother for her love of books and her father for her love of travel, but when she gripped a camera and pen for the first time, she found her two greatest loves—photography and writing.

An attorney in South Florida, she constantly juggles the demands of the law with those of writing. I-95 traffic jams are perfect for dictating tales of hard-fought love. She's thrilled that her debut as a published author is with Silhouette Special Edition. You can drop Carol a note at P.O. Box 1176, Boynton Beach, FL 33425-1176.

Rose Advice
by Connor Devlin

1. Tuck roses into your jacket lapel...and hers, too

2. Sprinkle rose petals atop your steaming hot
bathtub...and your bed

3. Build a rosebush nursery,
so you always have fresh roses at hand

4. Develop a new kind of rose...
and name it after the woman you love

5. Massage the woman you love
with freshly plucked rose petals...everywhere...

Prologue

Arcadia Heights, Ohio
Twenty years ago

Their hands.

When Abigail McCall opened the front door to her house, she first saw three pairs of hands, linked together across their bodies. So small, so fine, clamped white with tension.

Then, as she looked farther, she saw the three terrified pairs of eyes watching her above reddened cheeks. Three little girls joined together by blood and tragedy.

Abigail had been cursing the fates since she'd received the phone call yesterday. Her younger sister, Tess, had always been bent on destruction and had finally found it in a tawdry motel room. Thirty-five and dead of a drug overdose. Now the only evidence of

Tess's brief life was the three youngsters standing on Abigail's porch.

Tess had never cared about the bindings of marriage, had never stayed with the same man longer than a few months, had never bothered to protect herself. Her foolishness had produced three daughters by three different men. None of their fathers had come forward to claim the girls.

In the end, Tess's irresponsibility had come home to roost at her older sister's door. Abigail had been tempted to tell the social worker who called yesterday to take a hike. Why should she let Tess be the albatross around her neck again? Why should she pay the price for her sister's mistakes? She'd liked the life she'd made for herself in this small Midwest town, and she liked living alone.

But all thoughts of rejecting the girls shriveled and died the moment Abigail saw the poorly clothed little ones shivering before her. Their linked hands testified to their fear and their unified strength.

The tallest and eldest stood on the right, her thin shoulders hunched against the cold. Long black hair whipped around her pinched features.

On the other end, a pint-size blond angel waited patiently, her blue eyes wistfully fixed on the glowing light spilling from the front parlor onto the veranda's weathered planks.

Sandwiched between the two was the youngest child, who fidgeted until the oldest looked at her. The girl went still and stared, owl-eyed, at Abigail. Wisps of cinnamon-colored hair straggled out from under the brim of her blue knit cap. She lifted one joined pair of hands to wipe her nose. The older girl rolled her eyes but didn't let go, as if she feared someone would snatch her sister away.

Poor children. None of this was their doing.

Tears pricked Abigail's eyes. In that moment she lost her heart to them. Her nieces had suffered enough. It was time for them to have a real home.

Abigail dropped to her knees, silently encircling her nieces with her arms. Three heartbeats later, the blond pixie shyly put her free hand on Abigail's shoulder and frowned at her oldest sister. Eyes grayer than the November sky studied Abigail, judged her and came to a decision. The older girl's hand came up to rest on Abigail's shoulder. The smallest child, encapsulated by her sisters, flashed a dimpled smile and threw both hands around Abigail's neck.

They were hers now.

Three nights later, after the girls were asleep, Abigail carried a steaming mug of hot chocolate into her workshop at the rear of the house and went straight to her bench. During the summer months, she normally trekked across the backyard to her pottery shop, which faced the main business street. But with winter's unrelenting cold and wind, she retreated to a workshop set up in her converted den, which also accessed the back porch. Cocooned from the cantankerous weather, she worked her magic.

After unwrapping the plastic sheet from a block of ironware-grade clay, she placed the slab on the potter's wheel. After sluicing water over her hands, Abigail kneaded the clay, getting the feel of the formative powers of this particular lump. She closed her eyes and began to run her hands up and down the cool, moist material. Gradually she relaxed, the familiar tempo of molding the clay taking over all thought. Only instinct pulsed through her now.

The lump lifted, separated into three pieces. Experiencing only the sculpture, Abigail lost track of time. She scraped, she hollowed, she smoothed the pliable material. As she refined and refined again, her thoughts and prayers poured through her busy fingers into the clay.

Thoughts of love, prayers of hope, promises of forever—all worked into the core of the sculpture.

Finally Abigail stopped, spent, and wiped her clay-covered arm across her sleepy eyes. She dipped her aching hands into water, then wiped them with a towel. Biting her lower lip, she studied this newest piece of her heart.

From behind she heard a whispered exclamation of "Gosh!" She turned to find her nieces, dressed only in their pajamas, huddled together for warmth on the oak floor. The youngest, Eve, squirmed with excitement, restrained only by her sisters from getting up; the ethereal angel, Christina, glowed with inner fire as she studied the statuette. She looked at Abigail and said, "It's so beautiful."

Nora, the oldest one, solemnly studied the form without any visible reaction. She had been the last to eat, drink, bathe and go to bed each night. She'd always put her sisters first. To gain this trio's trust, Abigail knew she needed to win Nora's.

Rolling her head to relieve the kinks in her neck, Abigail smiled at the potential critic. "What do you think, Nora?"

The girl rose and walked to the wheel. Almost against her will, she reached out, then flushed red and stopped. "Whose hands are they?"

Abigail glanced at her work—three small hands, clasped together and raised, fragile fingers reaching toward the sky. She reached out and drew the child's stiff, resisting body to her side and rested her chin on the black silky hair.

"They are your hands, Nora. Yours and your sisters'."

"Why?" The child's voice was gruff. "Why did you bother to make our hands?"

"To remind you that the three of you will be bound together forever."

Suddenly the other sisters draped themselves over her knees. Christina's blue eyes were dreamy with enchantment. "Will it have a name? Like the other stuff you did?"

Abigail ran her hand over the soft, short cap of platinum hair. "Yes, Christina. I'm going to call it *Sisters Three.*"

Eve pursed her lips, her brown eyes surprisingly calculating in her six-year-old face. "Aunt Abigail, do you make lots of money?"

"Eve!" Nora glared at her sister, who grinned back, unrepentant.

Aunt. The word pulsed, shimmered in the air. Abigail swallowed a lump of emotion. None of them had called her that before. They were hers now, to protect, to raise, to love. And she would, until her dying breath.

"It's all right, Nora. We're a family now." She paused, spotting a brief flicker of hope in the oldest girl's eyes. Abigail wished she could chase away Nora's fears. She couldn't, not now, but she could nurture that spark of belief until one day it would vanquish the terror in her eyes.

To Eve she said, "I do all right with my pottery.

Good enough that tomorrow we're going shopping to buy you proper winter coats."

Christina beamed. "I want a purple coat."

"I want blue." Eve patted Abigail's knee for attention.

Abigail laughed. "I'm sure we can find a blue coat for you. How about you, Nora? What color do you like?"

Her stormy eyes too dark to reveal her thoughts, Nora shrugged. "It doesn't matter. My coat's okay. Eve and Christina need coats more."

Eve expectantly held up her arms. Abigail lifted the child onto her lap. The little girl leaned forward and whispered loudly, "Nora's always wanted a red coat, but Mama never had the money."

Abigail smiled. "Then red it is for Nora." She stroked Eve's cheek, marveling at the smooth, velvety texture. She noticed Nora studying the statue. "Well, sweetheart, do you like it or not?"

"It's missing one thing, Aunt Abigail." The girl turned toward them and held her hand palm up. Her sisters brought their hands up, leaving a space. Three expectant pairs of eyes stared at her. Her vision blurry, Abigail lifted her hand and completed the circle.

Chapter One

Arcadia Heights
The present

The clay figurine slipped from Nora McCall's numb fingers and exploded into a million pieces across the bare oak floorboards, shattering with it twelve years of Nora's carefully structured life. Her heart pounded with fear.

The tall man with eyes the color of a deep-blue sky entered the pottery shop. Only one male had that hell-bent-for-trouble walk, and that was Connor Devlin.

The very same man who was definitely heading her way.

Find Abby and hide, she thought as the blood roared in her ears. Instead, she stood, frozen by the man's determined gaze.

Her fingers flexed as she nervously glanced down at the floor. As she realized what she'd done a sensation of horror seeped through her.

Oh, no, she thought frantically. *Not Abby's cat.* Nora knelt and, heedless of the jagged edges, began scooping up the fragments. It was totaled. She'd never be able to glue it together again. Never.

Scuffed boot tips stopped before her.

Nora's hands stilled. One more crime to lay at Connor Devlin's feet—he'd destroyed her daughter's Mother's Day present.

"Hello, Nora."

She looked up. The wild, reckless boy of her dreams had turned into the dark, dangerous man of her nightmares. But he still wore the same rebel's uniform he had always worn: white T-shirt, second-skin blue jeans and trademark well-worn bomber jacket.

"What are you doing here?"

"You always could bring me to my knees, Nora McCall." Before she could rise and protect the precious pieces of Abby's cat, he crouched beside her, his hands brushing hers as he began picking up the broken pottery.

"Go away, Connor. I don't need *your* help," she snapped. She tried to nudge his hands aside, but he scooped up the last piece of clay. Frissons of awareness tingled along her arm, only to explode into raging resentment when he gripped her elbow and propelled her to her feet.

She broke free. Time had taken the boy's youth and replaced it with a man's face of sharp angles and planes. The once tall, rangy body had hardened into whipcord toughness. Windswept, sun-streaked chestnut hair fell over his brow and collar. Only his eyes were as she remembered—bold, piercing and purposeful.

He knew. He'd come for her.

"You look good. Just as I remembered you."

And he still had the ability to paralyze her—that stomach-quivering, breath-hitching, knee-jellying, mind-numbing power to immobilize with one curve of his mouth.

The shop bell chimed again, announcing visitors. Nora grabbed hold of her composure. This was their big day—the grand opening of Kilning You Softly—and she wouldn't let a ghost from her past ruin it.

She was no longer a young, impressionable girl who could be swayed by gorgeous eyes and a sexy mouth. Since her one life-altering mistake, she had avoided following her mother's path. The man before her meant nothing but trouble. He had no right to sashay into her store, into her life. Not after all this time.

She had to get rid of him.

The lawyer in her took over. "Why don't you get back on your knees and crawl out the way you came in."

Connor's nostrils flared slightly, and the corner of his mouth twitched. "Same old sassy mouth, too."

"My mouth is none of your business, Connor Devlin. Why are you here?" Needing space, she turned to the side and gently laid the pottery fragments on the hutch.

Connor moved to stand beside her. "Business." He held his hand over the wastepaper basket to throw out the shards.

Nora clutched his arm. "No! Don't!" She wrapped her fingers around his and pried at the shards. "Ow!"

She snatched her hand away and cradled it. Blood oozed from a jagged gash on the base of her left thumb.

Connor dumped the pieces on the sideboard. "Here, let me see that." His hand cupped hers.

Blinking away tears, Nora bent her head to get a closer look at the damage. Her forehead bumped Connor's. She bit back a curse as he gently probed the wound on her palm. The backs of his hands were broad and tanned, with a faint dusting of golden hair. She could feel the rough texture of his calluses as he wiped away the trail of blood. The hands of the boy were now the hard hands of a man. Whatever had happened to him, Connor still used his hands for a living.

Nora slanted a quick look at him through her wet lashes. His brow was furrowed as he checked her hand. Surreptitiously she leaned closer. Beyond the leather and soap, she could smell the sun and the earth clinging to him like an indelible part of his makeup.

Connor dragged a black bandanna from a pocket inside his jacket and wrapped it around the cut. "What was so important about that..." He glanced at the fragments and apparently couldn't divine their former existence. He shook his head. "Whatever it was, it wasn't worth slicing off a chunk of your finger. It's not as if it were irreplaceable like *The Sisters Three*."

No, it was only her daughter's attempt to console Nora over Aunt Abigail's death. It was every bit as precious to her as Abigail's most famous work, which glowed in its place of honor on the mantel in the store's rear alcove.

But Connor wouldn't know that. He wouldn't know about anniversaries, birthdays or deaths. After all, he hadn't been around for twelve years. Hadn't cared to be present. And now he had the audacity to lecture her in her own shop, filled with people she knew. People he'd scorned. The moment he knotted the fabric, she jerked her hand free and stepped away from him.

Irritation flashed across his face. "If you're worried about germs, that's a clean bandanna." He folded his arms. "I think you'll live, but you'd better have Doc Sims take a look at the cut to make sure you don't need stitches."

"I'm fine." And because Aunt Abigail had taught her better, she added, "Thanks." She looked down at her wrapped hand and caught sight of her watch. Almost eleven. She needed to get him out of the store. *Now.*

Her sisters, Christina and Eve, crossed to her, and she drew comfort from their presence. She would get through this, just as she had every other obstacle tossed in her path.

Nora McCall, standing proud, was a bittersweet image branded in Connor's memory. Once he had hoped to share his life with her, but that dream had never stood a chance. His pact with the devil, his mother, had seen to that.

Yet, over the years, doubt regarding his decision to leave town, to leave Nora, had snapped relentlessly at his conscience in the lonely hours when night met dawn. Now, seeing Nora and her sisters, a part of him felt at peace. The McCall girls were still together in a place they loved.

The devil had apparently kept her side of the bargain. She would not be pleased he was breaking his.

He nodded at the women. "Eve, Christina. Good to see you both." But he kept his gaze on Nora, even though every muscle in his body wound tighter. Tense as rectitude, his mother would have said.

Nora was still a knockout. From her lustrous black hair to her pressed jacket, she was all trim and lovely. And he had this craving to touch her, to feel once more the jolt of her pulse. If he had succumbed to his urge to press his lips against the soft flesh of her thumb while he had tended her wound, would he have found heat still running deep beneath her cool exterior?

The jab of desire irritated him, but Connor absorbed it. His gaze strayed to Nora's wrapped left hand. She wore no ring. If she hadn't married, would things have turned out different for them?

She arched a brow at his stare. "Gee, Connor, other than the mileage on your face, you haven't changed a bit. Very few older men can carry off that James Dean look. At least you've the good sense not to copy the hair."

Connor stiffened. A muscle jerked along his jaw. "You always did have brass, kid."

Her eyes narrowed dangerously. "I'm not a kid."

He slowly looked Nora up and down. "No, ma'am. You're certainly not."

Nora colored fiercely, but he gained only a grim pleasure from her discomfort. Why should he care about her? She certainly didn't care for him.

Shortly after he had left town, he had called his mother and said he couldn't go through with the deal. His tormentor had been silent for a second before crisply advising him to keep moving.

"Your high-and-mighty McCall girl got married last week." Even now, he could still hear the cold taunt that had ripped apart his soul.

Stunned, he had dropped the receiver and walked

away from the phone booth. Nora had run into another man's arms. She hadn't waited. She'd never pined for him.

So he had kept moving, seeking to put as much distance as possible between him and his past.

"Connor?"

He realized Christina had spoken.

"What?"

"I said we were all sorry about Ed Miller's passing."

The dull ache whenever he thought about the loss of the old man who had been his surrogate father throbbed. "Thanks."

Eve was brasher. "We figured you'd be there at the funeral."

"I couldn't get away." His jaw tensed. Missing Ed's service had torn him apart, but carrying out his promise to the farmer who had befriended him all those years ago had to come first. It wasn't until he'd gotten Ed's deathbed phone call that he'd learned he would finally get a chance to pay Ed back.

Nora accepted his statement without rebuke. "I'm sure you wanted to come, Connor. Ed was a good man."

"Yes, he was." More than anyone in the town would ever guess. Ed had been Connor's remaining link to his past, keeping him bound despite Connor's ending up in Florida. When Connor called Ed, the taciturn farmer had been circumspect about everything but his crops. Finally, desperate for news, Connor had asked the old man point-blank how Nora and her husband were doing. Ed had barked, "Husband. There's no husband."

Connor remembered his grim satisfaction in learning

of her divorce. However, he never could ferret out any additional information in subsequent calls to Ed. All the farmer would ever mutter was that "the McCall womenfolk were doing just fine."

He sure did miss the old coot.

Ever sensitive to other people's emotions, Christina said softly, "Pastor Devlin must be thrilled you've returned."

Pastor, not mother—Sheila Devlin would appreciate the distinction. She had certainly tried hard enough to distance herself from the role his birth had thrust on her. He hitched his shoulders. "She doesn't know I'm here. Yet."

Christina looked startled. "Oh." She huffed out a breath. "Well." Sadness flitted across her face. "Your mother performed a fine eulogy for Aunt Abigail."

Connor realized he hadn't offered condolences. He'd picked up the phone a hundred times when he had learned of their aunt's death. He'd replaced the receiver a hundred times because he hadn't known what to say.

He cleared his throat. "I can't tell you how sorry I was to hear about Abigail's death. She was a good woman." He gestured at the shop. "She'd be proud of what you've accomplished here."

Eve didn't mask her curiosity. "Thanks, Connor, but how did you—" The doorbell chimed. Eve narrowed her eyes.

A wave of new arrivals crowded around Nora and Christina. Breaking the crowd apart, Nathan Roberts, a tall lean man, sauntered past Eve, brushing so close that she had to step back to avoid contact. Watching the familiar byplay had Connor fighting to keep his lips flat. Some things never changed.

Nate crossed to Connor and clasped his hand. Behind wire-rim glasses, Nathan Roberts's slate-gray eyes warmed with amusement. "So, the town's favorite hell-raiser has returned. Will he receive a prodigal son's welcome?" He thumped Connor's shoulder.

Connor winced. "And you're still spouting off the biblical references." He studied his friend as they shook hands. Whatever life had chosen to throw Nate's way, it hadn't seemed to change him. His sandy hair was still shaggy from too-infrequent trips to the barbershop, his movements still languid as if he had all the time in the world.

Together, Nate and Connor had skipped stones across Miller's Lake as young boys, chugged down illicit beers at age eleven and discovered the allure of girls in high school. Nate had been a true friend and was the only local Connor was genuinely delighted to see.

Releasing Nathan's hand, Connor turned, cocked his head and curled his lip at the older man hovering behind his friend. "Nice to see you, too, Mr. Ames."

The high-school principal, without acknowledging the greeting, darted back into the shelter of the crowd. Nate chuckled. "He's never forgiven you for the time you set a skunk loose in his office."

Connor's grin was unrepentant. "It didn't have its odor sacs."

"A pity Ames didn't realize that little fact before he pulled the fire alarm, bringing the entire department racing to the school. It was a day to remember."

Connor shifted to keep Nora within his line of sight. At that moment she tucked a loose strand of hair behind her ear. An intense awareness jolted through his system. He remembered the intriguing spot on her body where warm, soft skin contrasted with cool, silky hair.

Nora looked up and caught him staring. Irked with himself, he offered a bland smile. She shot him a withering look and turned her back.

Even as Connor fell into easy conversation with Nate about their past adventures, he continued to torment himself with the tantalizing vision of the long graceful sweep of Nora's neck.

On the other side of the shop, Nora was suffocating, the weight of suppressed, raw emotions pressing all air from her lungs. If one more person made a cutting comment about Connor, she would scream. She had to escape.

She glanced around and spotted Connor and Nate deep in discussion. Connor rubbed his knuckles along his deeply shadowed jaw. Fascinated, she remembered the rasp of his developing whiskers. How would his face, roughened with manhood, feel against hers? Connor looked across and caught her staring. A smile, slow and cocky, curved his mouth. Her cheeks heated as if she was standing too close to the kiln.

The two men broke apart, and Connor plowed into the crowd, heading in her direction. No, she couldn't bear any more polite conversation with him while half the town watched. She bolted for the front door.

Outside she drank in the fragrant air. Deep breathing, a technique she had learned to calm pretrial jitters, slowly untangled the knots in her stomach. She rolled her head and stilled, the sky capturing her attention.

White plumes of cloud drifted across the achingly blue October sky. She lifted her face and took another bracing breath of frost-edged air, laced with woodsy overtones.

Her gaze lowered. Chased by the playful fall wind, crisp leaves of orange, red and yellow skipped merrily along the tree-lined street. Normally this was her favorite time of year, when autumn muscled aside Indian summer. The scene before her should have calmed her, but didn't. Change was snapping at her heels, threatening to devour her, yet Arcadia Heights remained the same on the outside. It wasn't fair.

Today should have been perfect.

The door behind her opened, crushing her solitude.

Nora warily watched Wilbur Ames march out, heading determinedly toward her. She cast a desperate look around her, but milling shoppers blocked her escape. No matter that she was a grown-up and an attorney, her old high-school principal could still reduce her to teenage status. Nora steeled herself.

"Thank you for dropping by, Mr. Ames. On your way?"

Jowly from one too many potluck dinners, Ames's face was ruddy with exertion. The drapes of his flesh quivered with indignation. "I can't believe that Connor Devlin has returned. His poor mother will be horrified."

The insult to Connor irritated Nora, but she quelled her feelings. She might as well hear Wilbur's tirade out. Wilbur's washed-out blue eyes darted nervously about. "I saw him in the corner talking to his partner in crime." Ames's contempt was palpable. "We'll have nothing but trouble with Connor in town. The boy broke his mother's heart with all his hell-raising."

Sheila Devlin never had a heart, especially not where her son was concerned. Even when the minister had stepped in and helped the McCall family in their time of need, Nora hadn't been able to shake the sense that the woman had done it out of self-interest, rather than kindness. Remembering the extent of the obligation she owed the woman sent a chill down Nora's spine. To date, Pastor Devlin had rebuffed all attempts to repay the debt. It was as if she was waiting to exact the perfect price.

Although Nora knew Wilbur would carry any comment straight to Sheila Devlin, she couldn't ignore the injustice to Connor, even if it meant tipping the scales of her uneasy relationship with his mother. "It's been almost twelve years since our class graduated from high school." Her voice carried only the mildest rebuke. "We've all changed. We've all grown up."

Ames's beady eyes glinted with interest as he studied her. "Weren't you two involved before he left town?" His tongue flicked out and ran over his protruding lips.

Of course he knew. It was why he had made a beeline for her. Wilbur Ames never forgot anything, particularly the juicy transgressions of others.

Nora laughed lightly. She'd give him a little of the truth to take away his joy in the dirt. "What a long memory you have, Mr. Ames. Of course, I went out a few times with him. After all, what girl didn't Connor date?"

His hungry eagerness deflated. "Yes, of course. Not that it was my business. Anyway, nice to see you again and congratulations on the pottery shop." The principal turned to leave.

"By the way, Mr. Ames."

He paused.

"Have you and the school board had a chance to consider my suggestion about the girls' soccer field?"

"Not yet. We have a full agenda."

"I'm sure you do, but the girls are playing—"

"Now, Nora. We appreciate your school spirit and

such, but we'll get to it all in due time." He turned and walked off.

"You handled Wilbur well—right up until the end where he gave you the brush-off."

Nora's heart shot into her throat and performed a back flip at Connor's rough voice. She slowly turned her heart pounding again. Connor stood with one shoulder braced against the gray clapboard front of the store.

Keep it light and general, she told herself, and maybe he won't ask why she was interested in a girls' soccer field. She shrugged and smiled in a what-can-you-do manner.

"An old community issue that he continues to ignore."

"What a shocker. Wilbur Ames's not seeing anything beyond his own self-interest. Some things never change." Connor folded his arms. "I guess I should thank you for your spirited defense of me." He studied her, his piercing gaze bright with speculation.

No. She couldn't afford to have Connor think she still harbored any feelings for him. "It's why I became an attorney. I enjoy a good verbal challenge."

Something flickered in his eyes—disappointment?—but when he straightened, it was gone.

"Looks like your store's a big hit."

Satisfaction shone in Nora as she surveyed Kilning You Softly. After months of backbreaking scrubbing, refurbishing and polishing, she and her sisters had succeeded in making their tribute to their aunt a reality. Last night, as the final touch, they had placed *Three Sisters* on the gray marble mantel over the fireplace. There, under soft recessed lighting, the glazed pink fig-

urine of three small hands glowed serenely in testament
to all that Abigail McCall had given.

Now it was Nora's duty to ensure her home remained intact. She gnawed on her lower lip.

A muffled groan startled her. A dismayed Connor
stood beside her.

"Are you all right?" Nora asked.

He smiled ruefully, but he only nodded at the building. "I take it Christina picked out the colors."

Both the shutters and the lettering on the sign over
the doorway were a jaunty purple. Nora winced. "I
missed the appointment with the painter."

"I hear Christina's going to run the place."

Unease prickled across the nape of Nora's neck.
"You've heard an awful lot in a very short period of
time."

His response was an enigmatic smile. Nora's unease
ripened into panic. *Why was he here?*

She wrapped her arms around herself and turned
away from his piercing stare. What did he know? Was
he playing a cruel game of hide-and-seek with her?

When Ed Miller had died a month ago, she had been
certain that Connor would return. After all, the farmer
had been like a father to him. Her tension in the days
leading up to the funeral had been worse than any trial
nerves. But Connor never came. A lavish arrangement
of yellow roses and a simple card delivered to Ed's
grave had been Connor's only acknowledgment of the
man's passing. The townspeople had branded him for
his disrespect, but Nora had been relieved.

Ed Miller. Nora thought of the sealed envelope in
her briefcase. It contained documents for the unknown
Miller heir, given to her by her boss, Charles Barnett,
to deliver at noon today. She'd gathered from Barnett's

hints the new owner was a wealthy businessman and a lucrative new account. But Charlie had been tight-lipped about the heir's identity.

Nora stole a glance at Connor's worn jeans and jacket. It looked like the success he had hungered for had eluded him, but the roses for Ed's service couldn't have been cheap.

Roses. Abigail's funeral. A memory tugged free. Two dozen sweetheart roses, each blossom a perfect deep-red velvet, had graced her aunt's church service. The accompanying card had borne no signature, just the typed words "To a great woman."

Nora swung around. "Connor, did you send flowers—"

He interrupted her. "I have to be going."

Disappointment sliced through her.

Ridiculous. His leaving was what she wanted. She mustered a cool, professional smile. "How long will you be staying in town?"

Connor tucked his hands in the front pockets of his jeans and rocked on his heels. "Well, now. That question implies I'm only visiting."

Nora stiffened, her heart hammering wildly, the blood humming in her ears. "What do you mean?" she asked as casually as she could manage. "Aren't you just passing through?" She almost shrank back under the burning challenge in his eyes.

His tone, though, was chillingly calm. "No. I've come back to stay."

The humming became a roar. *He was staying.*

The door to the shop slammed.

A tall slender girl, poised on the edge of her teens, rushed outside. "Hey, Mom! Do you know where my jersey is? I've looked everywhere.'' Close behind her were Eve and Christina, both looking anxious.

Nora's gaze locked with Connor's. ''Have you tried the laundry room? It's folded on top of the dryer.''

Her daughter threw her arms around Nora's neck and gave her a quick peck. ''Mom, you're the best.'' Turning, she noticed Connor and immediately trotted out her practiced smile, designed to slay the male population. ''Hi, I'm Abby.''

Nora saw the stunned but puzzled look in Connor's eyes as he shook the proffered hand. Relief flowed through her. Her sisters gripped her arms, keeping her from sagging.

He didn't know.

He had not known.

Standing before Connor was Nora, a girl again. But not Nora.

Her daughter. He could barely form the word mentally. The girl was the spitting image of her mother, all coltish long limbs. Connor blinked and took a closer look at Abby. No. There were some physical differences. Abby's black hair was wavy; a hint of a dimple winked at the right corner of her mouth when she smiled; her eyes were the blue of a tropic sky, not the wintry gray of her mother's.

Did she have her father's eyes? Jealousy sliced through Connor. Nora had a child by another man. During all those long Florida nights, filled with restive dreams of Nora, he'd never once envisioned her as a mother.

Weary from fending off all the emotional punches he'd sustained in the space of thirty minutes, Connor rotated his shoulders. It wasn't the first time he'd had to cut his losses and move on, and it probably wouldn't be the last. The memory of the special gift Nora had given him was only that—a memory.

Connor realized Abby was studying him with the same intense concentration that her mother displayed, right down to the identical furrowing of dark brows. Despite himself, he smiled. The girl's responding grin yanked loose one of the knots in his stomach.

"I'm Connor Devlin. I knew your mother when she looked just like you." He waited a beat. Yep, here came the trademark McCall rolling of eyes. No one else had ever been able to do it with the same expressiveness as Nora. "And she was the prettiest girl in her class," he smoothly continued. "So were your aunts. All major babes. Boys stumbled over themselves to catch sight of a McCall in the hallway."

Abby turned and looked incredulously at the woman standing behind her. "My mother? A babe?"

Grimacing, Nora stepped away from her sisters and ran a hand over her daughter's cheek. "Connor, hush. You'll spoil my daughter's image of me as a proper old woman."

He looked at Nora's open jacket, revealing her subtle curves. If she was old, then someone needed to put him out of his misery right then and there. The sudden need to feel the cool silk of Nora's shirt against his chest before he explored the warm flesh beneath left him on edge. He'd thought his need for Nora had died years ago, yet the slow heat in his groin had him shifting his stance.

"Oh, Mom!" Abby straightened, all teenage righteous indignation. "Come on!"

Eve's mouth curled. "Babes, huh?"

Connor stepped forward and pulled on one of Eve's curls. "Babes then, babes now." Eve flushed and jerked her head away. He winked, and Eve's jaw dropped.

Pleased, Connor moved to Christina and lightly pressed her hand. "Good to see you, Christie." His reward was a lightening of the haunted shadows in her eyes.

He next tugged Abby's ponytail. "Nice to meet you." Warmth unfurled in him when she smiled.

Connor then stood before Nora and took her injured hand. A test, for old time's sake. Just a harmless test. When he turned it over and kissed the pulse at her wrist, the soft flesh jolted. Hot triumph burned through him—she still reacted to his touch.

Unfortunately his body reacted in kind.

Stepping back, he nodded. "Ladies, it's been a pleasure." He turned and strolled down the sidewalk.

He had reached the next line of stores when Nora called out, "You weren't serious about staying here permanently, were you?"

His step almost faltered. Everyone's anxiousness to see him gone, especially Nora's, angered him. He should set the record straight.

He looked over his shoulder. Did he imagine the flicker of panic in her eyes? He still felt contrary enough to let the half-truth stand—for now. "Very serious."

He reached his pride-and-joy, a gleaming Harley-Davidson Fat Boy motorcycle, and straddled it. As he cinched on his helmet, he delivered his parting shot. "I'll be seeing you around."

Nora gaped.

After a careless salute, Connor revved the bike's engine and roared off down the road. Next up, his meeting with the devil.

Chapter Two

The old church hunkered on the windswept hill at the west end of Maple Street. A third-generation building, it stood on the foundation of its predecessors. When the first two structures had succumbed to fire, no one had dared to move the location of the First Community Church of Arcadia Heights.

No minister had guarded the First Community Church tradition more zealously than its current minister: the town's first female pastor.

The first thing that struck Connor as he sat on his motorcycle in front of the church was how little it had changed. Its clapboard still glared pristine white under the late-morning sun. Its steeple was a stark pillar thrusting upward to pierce the blue plane of the autumn sky. The steeple could be seen for miles. When its bells clanged on Sunday morning, few could escape their imperious summons.

Connor kicked down the bike stand and slung his helmet over the handlebar. He ran his fingers through his hair and tucked in his T-shirt. He walked along the bricked sidewalk. At the path's split, rather than taking the steps to the church's entrance, he veered to the right. At this time on Saturday, if the keeper of the faith maintained her ritual, she'd be polishing her Sunday sermon in the cottage's study. His practiced eye noted the stern, cropped lines of the viburnum hedges along the perimeter of the church. He knew the shrubs weren't pruned just for the oncoming winter. Come spring, no twig would be permitted to sprout its spectacular white flowers.

He turned the corner and faced the place where he had grown up. Reaching the pine-green-painted door, he opted to rap his knuckles rather than use the imposing brass knocker. He counted the seconds it would take the resident to rise from her chair and cross the hallway.

The door swung out, and a tall woman with a smile that didn't quite mask her annoyance stood in the entrance's shadows. "I'm sorry, but could you please come back later when..." Her lips thinned with displeasure. "Connor. What are you doing here?"

Because he knew it would irritate her, he leaned forward and brushed his lips across the woman's cheek. "Hello, Mother. Nice to see you, too."

She grimaced and, with her hand on the knob, retreated a step into the dim shadows of the entryway.

"Don't bother inviting me in." Connor leaned against the doorjamb, keeping one foot extended in case she tried to shut the door in his face.

Sheila Devlin folded her hands in front of her body

and studied him. "I see you haven't changed. Still look like a third-rate hooligan."

Her disapproval, though expected, was a painful reminder of the abuse she once inflicted. "Thanks, Mom. I wish I could say the same for you." He returned the survey. Gray hairs, like shards of ice, speared through her auburn hair. This sign of mortality only served to enhance his mother's air of authority. Her aquiline nose and frosty blue eyes bespoke her Irish heritage, but the fine lines radiating from her full lips signaled rigid self-control. She wore her uniform of black tailored slacks, crisp Oxford buttoned-down shirt and polished black loafers.

She arched a well-shaped patrician brow. "I assume your return has to do with Ed Miller's death, but you're a little late. His funeral was a month ago."

He shrugged. "There are other ways to pay one's last respects."

"What?" His mother was the only person he'd ever known who could snort with elegance. "Uproot a flower in his honor?"

Her barb, as intended, sliced deep, but Connor merely rubbed his chin. "What a great idea. Thanks, Mother." He straightened. "I came by to let you know I'm here and will be staying at Ed's farm."

His movement allowed a shaft of sunlight to stream into the hallway and fall short at his mother's feet.

"Why?"

"Because Ed left me the place, and I have plans for it." Motes danced in the sunbeam. Funny, when he had been growing up, Sheila had kept the rooms white-glove clean. He didn't recall her allowing even one speck of dust to occupy the same space with her. She certainly hadn't permitted a young boy's toys.

"What plans could you possibly have?"

He jammed his hands into his pockets. Better than ramming one into the wood frame. "Nothing to interest you. Just a landscaping business."

"Still into dirt." The motes scattered as if they could sense the derision emanating from her. "Have you seen *her?*"

Trust his mother to get right to the point. Connor set his jaw. "Yes."

"We had a deal."

And he had never been able to sweat off the weight of his wretched promise under the unrelenting sun of Florida. His voice was rough. "Never fear, Mother. It's over for both of us. I met Nora's daughter." He doubted if he would have any success of working this particular ache out of his system this afternoon.

His mother laced her fingers. Despite the fact she couldn't hurt him anymore, the gesture sent a chill racing along his spine. As a child, he'd learned that the linking of her fingers signaled her more violent outbursts. His gaze flicked up to her face; some emotion darkened her eyes momentarily. Then her face resumed its expressionless mask. "Good." She hesitated. "I do hope your 'plans' won't take you long."

Connor removed his foot from the opening. "Your welcome is overwhelming."

He wouldn't have thought it possible, but his mother's posture became even more rigid. "I'm up for a promotion to a higher office. A much more affluent parish."

His smile was rueful. "And you're worried that my return will screw up your chances for 'exalted-dom.'"

Her chin lifted. "Crude as always, but accurate."

He turned on his heel. "Not to worry, Pastor Devlin.

I'll try not to lay too many sins at your door. Now if you'll excuse me, I have an appointment to keep with Nora about legal matters.''

He went down the porch steps.

''Connor!'' The unfamiliar note of anxiety brought him around in surprise. Sheila's emotions normally lay dormant, except when she preached. His mother ventured into the sunlight. ''There's nothing for you here. Certainly not that McCall girl. If you try to take up with her, you'll just ruin her life.''

His hands clenched in his pockets. Keep them there, he warned himself. ''How do you figure that?''

''She's seeing Lawrence Millman's son.''

''David?''

''Yes. The whole town's expecting the engagement notice any time now.''

Her words only made his flame of longing for Nora burn brighter. He hitched his shoulders. ''Good. I'm happy for them.'' He moved. He needed to get to the farm and weed through his tangle of thoughts and emotions.

''Connor!''

He paused again, but didn't turn around this time.

''It would be best if you left town now.''

He shook his head. ''That's where you're wrong, Mother. I have an obligation to fulfill.''

''What do you know about obligation?''

He looked over his shoulder and looked into eyes devoid of any maternal love. ''More than you. While you were busy ministering to your congregation, you shucked your duty to raise me.''

He ignored her gasp and walked around the corner of the church.

Nora's Mercury Sable groaned, its undercarriage scraping on the deep dip in the dirt track. She gritted her teeth and eased her foot off the gas pedal. The car's forward momentum was due more to sheer pitching of its wheels from rut to rut than from the engine. Whoever the unlucky heir to the Miller farm, he would be forced to spend a mint paving this nonexistent driveway. With a final shudder, her car lurched around the bend and halted in the clearing.

Nora rested her forehead on the steering wheel, needing a few moments to compose herself. If she'd had half a brain, she would have heeded Eve's suggestion and cut through the woods between their house and the Miller farm. A ten-minute walk on a well-trodden trail—that was all it would have taken. Eve had dryly suggested she lower herself to wear jeans and sneakers and actually enjoy the fall colors in the process of her visit.

But no, Nora had insisted that she needed to be professional. What new client would want to see his lawyer emerging all burr-covered from a forest? Eve's mockingly raised eyebrow had sent her in a huff from the house, then over that miserable pitted track.

All because ghosts had awakened in those woods. Shadowy memories stirred by the flash-in-the-pan appearance of Connor Devlin. That was all it would be, too. She wouldn't, couldn't, fool herself, despite his puzzling parting comment. With a swagger and a grin, he was here today; without a look back, he'd be gone tomorrow. Just like he had been twelve years ago, without a thought for the consequences of his actions.

Well, she'd lived with those consequences, sacrificing herself to them. She would not feel guilty about decisions made a dozen years ago. The specters of youthful dreams and promises could lurk and linger in that bank of trees. She was in control of her life and would remain so.

Yeah, right, she thought. If she was in so much control, why did she feel eighteen, perched on the slippery precipitous edge of ruin once again? She could still recall the sweat trickling down her back that hot summer day when she had told Abigail. She had been so scared her aunt would turn against her in disgust. After all, wasn't she just like her mother? Pregnant with no husband? But Abigail had opened her arms and her heart once more.

Now the father of her child had returned. What had he meant by his *I'll be seeing you around?* Did he think he could take up where he left off?

She lightly thumped her brow against the wheel. Right now she needed to pull herself together before she met with her law firm's newest source of income. Nora raised her head and studied the farmhouse. It was a big box of a place, two-story, with a steep-pitched roof and central chimney. Snuggled against the forest's edge, the dwelling bore its dingy white siding, peeling forest-green shutters and dilapidated wraparound porch with quiet dignity. Yet, in the harsh noon light, its high narrow windows glistened, no doubt due to a recent application of elbow grease and glass cleaner. A sign of hope.

Hope, in the form of whoever owned the outrageous Ford F-350 parked in front. Big, bad and black—every boy and man's fantasy pickup, topped off with gleaming chrome wheels and bumpers, an extended cab and dark-tinted glass. She would bet a dollar the interior was a wicked red leather.

Clean windows and made-for-sin truck. What kind

of a man had Ed Miller left his spread to? She wouldn't find any answers sitting there. Nora got out of the car and grabbed her leather portfolio. Hugging it close to her body, she hesitated. She couldn't resist—she had to know. In case the owner was watching from inside the house, she made her way around the clearing, out of sight of the house, to the truck. She took a quick peek inside. Her lips curved. Yep, red-hot leather interior.

A muttered oath came from the far side of the building. Nora stepped carefully over the dirt surface to the grass, mentally ignoring the fact that her good leather pumps were sinking into the soggy turf.

She looked up, and stopped still. What once had been an expanse of green lawn was now freshly turned earth with roped-off areas. Shallow ditches contained pipes leading to one section, while nearby, a tarp covered huge translucent panels. Ed Miller's pride and joy, a battered old American Harvester tractor, stood to one side, hitched to a tiller. But it was the moving forms that captured Nora's attention.

A giant dog, its long black fur gleaming with a reddish sheen, picked up a stone, padded across the soil and dropped the rock on a pile at the side. Then it turned its massive head and studied Nora with chocolate-brown eyes. Nora braced herself to call for help, but the animal, with a smooth rhythmic gait, returned to the churned earth, sat and waited.

By the dog's side worked a shirtless man, his back to her. The man's powerful, well-muscled body moved with graceful ease as he yanked loose a large stone and tossed it toward the pile. He stretched to scratch the dog behind its ear. When he bent over once more to grip another rock, Nora spotted a tantalizing glimpse of even more skin. Sun-kissed flesh. All over his hard body. The image sizzled, so hot she almost unfastened the top button of her shirt. She gasped softly for air.

The man shot up and spun around. ''What's the matter, Nora? Having a hot flash?'' Squinting against the sun, Connor grinned, slowly and wickedly.

Belatedly Nora spotted the motorcycle parked nearby.

Flash, no. Conflagration, yes. The boy she had known had grown up. Damp burnished hair covered the solid wall of his chest, tapering across his flat stomach before disappearing below his belt line. She glanced downward…and caught herself. Her cheeks burning, Nora cast a veiled look at Connor.

''So the ice goddess has mortal thoughts, after all.'' His expression was dark, hungry. His eyes slid down her body, moving languidly, assessing her in turn. She shivered under his intense scrutiny.

Forgotten feelings, long frozen, sparked, flickered and spread like wildfire inside her. Want, need, desire. Too long leashed, they shot victoriously to her core.

Nora put a trembling hand over her abdomen. She yearned to touch all that glorious golden skin, slide her palms over the faint sheen of sweat on those wide shoulders. Connor's strangled sound, half growl, half longing, summoned her. His intense gaze drew her in like a powerful undertow, ever closer to his heat. She felt she would incinerate if she didn't break free. Summoning all her resolve, she wrenched her gaze away. She glanced at her watch. Ten minutes past twelve. The time was as effective as a cold shower on her roiling emotions.

Oh, Lord, what was she doing? The Miller heir could come outside any second.

"Put your shirt on," she snapped. Rushing to where it was draped over a twisted tree stump, she picked it up and tossed it to him. "The new owner is a client of my firm, and I don't want him imagining any funny business going on."

The dog rose slowly; the movement edged her back a step. Connor placed a hand on the animal's broad head and murmured, "She's okay, Bran." With that reassurance, the dog turned, picked up a small rock with its mouth and moved toward the pile.

Connor swiped the shirt across his brow without putting it on. "What's wrong, Nora?" he asked, all innocence.

She gritted her teeth. "Nothing's wrong. I just prefer my first meeting with my client to remain professional rather than Chippendales."

Connor arched an eyebrow. "Somehow I think there's a backhanded compliment in there."

Nora stomped her foot. "Just put on your shirt."

"Only if it will make you more comfortable, honey." He slowly, very slowly, pulled it on, then raked his fingers through his hair.

She scanned the back of the house. "What are you doing here?" She recalled a comment her boss had made earlier in the week about employing cleaning help for the homestead. "Did Charlie hire you to do repairs?" Maybe she should go to the front entrance and knock.

"Can't see the present for the past, can you?"

Before Nora realized what was happening, Connor stepped up and took her hand. "I'm the new owner."

Her mouth dropped open. "Wha-what did you say?" Her voice was barely a whisper, so fragile it cracked.

"Ed Miller left me the farm."

Realizing he still held her hand, she tugged it free. "How can that be possible? Why you?"

Connor shrugged, bent down and plucked a wild flower from a tall spiky plant. He slipped the deep-red blossom through a hole on the lapel of her jacket. "Remember how I used to work summers and weekends for Mr. Miller?"

She nodded and fingered the flower. The memory of another time, another flower, pierced her heart.

"Yes, I remember."

A white rose. The last night she had been with Connor, he had given her the snow-white bud. Her first flower from a boy. Her hands had trembled, and she'd pricked her finger. He had cupped her hand, sucking gently on the drop of blood, his mouth warm and tantalizing against her skin.

Nora closed her eyes and clamped down on her rioting emotions. No, she would not let his spontaneous gesture of picking a flower weaken her resolve. She lifted her head, opened her eyes.

Connor shoved his hands into his jean pockets. "Ed and his wife never had any kids of their own, and none of his relatives cared about the farm. He used to complain about that while we were out in the field." For a moment he smiled with the memory. Then his expression became remote. "Anyway, after Ed passed away, Barnett contacted me and said the old man had left everything in my trust."

Nora took a deep calming breath. Perhaps he'd only returned to sell the spread. "But there's barely any money with the estate, just the land. How are you going to pay the property taxes? Or are you selling it as soon as you can?"

Anger flaring in his eyes, Connor went from relaxed

to battle alert. Nora took a half step back before stopping herself.

"You sure have changed, haven't you, Nora? Prepared to think the worst of me like everyone else in this town." She heard the pain rippling beneath the ice in his voice.

She had hurt him. Funny, she'd always thought no one could penetrate Connor's armor. The boy she hadn't understood was now a man she didn't know. She flushed and gestured, indicating the farm. "But it's 165 acres."

Connor hitched his shoulders slightly. "So?" His tone was belligerent. "Do you think I can't afford it? Pastor Devlin's no-account son ran off to be a failure?"

His accusation hit Nora squarely. He was right. Part of her wanted to believe the worst about him. How else could she reconcile the cold truth that he hadn't told her he was leaving, hadn't contacted her in all this time?

She narrowed her eyes. "How should I know? How would I know anything about you? You left this town and didn't look back, remember?" He hadn't been there for her during those moments of terrifying need. Pain may have lost its sharp edge, but resentment could still carve deep.

She drew in a steadying breath before continuing. "You didn't write, you didn't call. For all I knew, you were dead."

Liar, her inner voice whispered. *If something had happened to him, you would have felt it.*

Surprise flickered in his eyes. His smile mocked her. "I'm sure my mother would have broadcast the glad tidings of my death." He paused, his face hardening. "Besides, wouldn't it have been awkward if I called?

The husband you snagged the moment I left might have objected.''

Nora blinked. That wasn't the tale she and Aunt Abigail had molded. When had the lie of a college misadventure transmuted into one of marriage? Like a kaleidoscope, the fragments of her life shifted and formed a new realization. She almost staggered under its weight.

There was not going to be any escape from this quandary. She was going to have to tell him the truth. Then the town would hear. And...

Abby. Oh, God, what would the news do to her daughter? When Abby had been old enough to ask questions, Nora had spun the story of an ill-fated college romance and her decision to have the baby. If told the truth, would Connor disappear again? What would that do to Abby?

No. She needed more time to assess the man standing before her. Her daughter's future was at stake.

She drew herself up, summoned her reserve of calm and looked straight at him. ''You're mistaken. I was never married.''

''But she told me...'' His eyes narrowed with suspicion. ''Your daughter, Abby,'' he said carefully. ''Is she...?''

Her heart hammered so loudly she feared he would hear it. She affected a nonchalant shrug. ''The result of a failed romance. I met this boy and fell in love, but he wasn't ready to become a man. He left me, and I've never heard from him since.''

God help her, she couldn't resist the taunt that hissed up from her turbulent emotions. ''Leaving town rather than facing responsibility seems to be a male proclivity.''

Connor's expression darkened. His hands lashed out and yanked her against his body, his fingers digging into her shoulders.

"How dare you compare me to him!" His arms slid around her like a vise. "Didn't what we shared mean anything to you?"

It had meant everything to her. "No."

He drew her closer. They were flesh to flesh. Her senses overflowed with him. He was earth and sweat, muscle and power. Heat. Roaring, incendiary heat. She couldn't inhale without breathing in his scent.

"No?" He lowered his head. "Then it won't mean anything if you kiss me."

"Cut it out." She spread her hands against his muscled chest.

"Why?" His breath fanned her face. "It's only a kiss."

An image flashed into her mind, of her intoxicated mother giggling as she tussled with her latest leering paramour. He had pawed her mother, saying, "Give me a kiss, Tess." After a few coy protests, her mother had lustily complied. "Get rid of the kids," the man had ordered as he staggered into their mother's bedroom. Tess had dragged the girls into their room, with Nora fighting all the way because they hadn't eaten.

The snick of the closet-door lock. The taste of fear.

"Nora, take it easy. Look at me."

With a start, Nora realized she was struggling in his arms.

"Breathe," he ordered.

Shame smothered her panic and she stilled.

"Are you okay?" He eased his grip. She fought to take a normal breath. With a light touch, he ran his hands up and down her arms. Her tension ebbed with each stroke; in its place drifted comfort and something else…a stirring of the blood. She sighed.

"Nora?" Connor bent down and pressed his forehead to hers. "I'm sorry for upsetting you, honey."

Flustered, Nora stepped back. Too many secrets prevented even this closeness. "Thanks. I'm fine."

Connor dropped his hands. "All right." He ran his fingers through his hair. "Look. I'm…sorry for what I said about Abby's father." Nora almost smiled. She didn't recall him ever apologizing, let alone twice in one conversation.

"What's done is done. I have no business prying." He bent down, picked up her briefcase and handed it to her. His fingertips brushed hers, sending another ripple of warmth through her.

The dog appeared at his side, and Connor absently ruffled his head.

Nora eyed the beast. "Big dog."

"He's a Newfoundland. Bran—" he gestured at her "—I want you to meet Nora."

On cue, the dog lifted his right paw. Nora knelt and solemnly shook it. "It's a pleasure to meet you, Bran." It was all the encouragement Bran needed. He surged forward and gave her a generous lick on her face, the force of it knocking her backward. Only Connor's hands under her arms saved her from a close encounter with the churned soil. With an ease that left her humming, Connor righted her. For a moment they stood, flushed face to flushed face.

Connor looked away first. "So." In fascination she watched the flex of the muscle along his lean jaw. "Why don't I show you how I plan to turn this place into a landscaping and nursery outlet, and what I'm going to need in terms of legal know-how?"

Lost in a whirlpool of emotions and questions, Nora tried to catch hold of the conversation. "What outlet?"

"The Primal Rose." Connor turned and smiled with undisguised pride. "Follow me." He gestured toward the fields.

Just like old times, Nora mused. Picking up her briefcase, she caught the now-crushed flower in her lapel.

Connor Devlin was starting a business here. He really had come home to stay.

Oh, God, what was she going to do?

Chapter Three

Late Saturday night Nora's flashlight cast a thin yellow line into the dark forest that ran between her house and the Miller farm. No branches rattled, no animals rustled. It was not a night for anything living to be about, yet the whispers of memories drew her deeper into the woods.

A cloak of clouds pressed close to the treetops. The still shroud smothered the night sky, rendering it flat. It was as if there were only two planes—the clouds and the earth—and all that dared to intervene did so at their peril.

Panic's wings stirred and fluttered, but Nora kept her gaze glued to the faint illumination. Each step along this path covered a moment of her life: a child's escape from nightmares; a teenager's captivation with adventure; a woman's dreams shattered by heartache.

She remembered the first weekend after she and her

sisters had arrived in Arcadia Heights. A snowstorm had dressed the bleak landscape in a white glittering cape. In wonderment, Nora had stood at the edge of the yard, outfitted in her new red winter coat. Familiar only with the ins and outs of city apartments, she hadn't known what lay beyond the sentry of trees.

Aunt Abigail had found her and had coaxed her into the forest. At this bend Nora had encountered her first deer, a doe with soulful brown eyes. On that old pine tree, Abigail had shown her how moss grew. Nora had taken to the woods, transfixed by this mysterious new world. It was on one of her daily excursions that she'd discovered her special retreat.

Still, her visits had been restricted to daylight. Only one person had drawn her out into the night and shown her its unique magic.

Connor Devlin.

With him, the trees had rubbed their branches in harmony to the lake's soft music. With him, there had been no twilight fear, just the thrill of laughter and freedom. When he had left, the darkness once more had ceased to be safe. She had not ventured into the night again. Until now.

This Saturday evening, penitence drove her past the good memories to those hidden in the blackest shadows. Guilt lingered on the edge of her conscience, out of sight but not out of mind. All her life she had stood tall, but shame had almost brought her to her knees this afternoon. Still, she hadn't told Connor about Abby. Couldn't—not when so many questions remained unanswered.

Who *was* this man who had fathered her daughter? Would he become a part of his child's life? Or would he desert her the way he had deserted her mother?

Abby. She'd never known abandonment, never felt the fear. For her a closet was just a place to hang clothes; sunset was merely the end of a day. Her daughter didn't know the bitter bite of betrayal. She didn't know about the monsters that came with nightfall.

But Nora did.

The flashlight beam hit a wall of brush, and she halted. The path broke into two long dark tunnels. One led to the Miller farm, the other to the lake. She glanced to her left, and her breath hitched. Rather than a corridor of trees, she saw a never-ending closet, ink-black with no means of escape.

Was the pounding in her ears her heart beating? Or the sound of a terrified child's fists against a locked door?

A small whimper welled in her throat and broke past her clenched teeth. Nora spun around and ran back toward the only real home she'd ever known.

The cry of pain brought Bran to an alert stance and Connor to a stop. Was it animal or human? Then he heard soft footfalls ahead of him and to his left. He hefted the large flashlight, securing his grip on it, and rushed forward, the dog in an easy lope beside him. When he reached the fork, he panned the beam along the path leading to the McCall house.

Nothing. Several inches of pine needles covered the trail. There were disturbed areas, but he couldn't tell whether they were recent.

He hesitated. He should mind his own business and continue to the lake as he had planned. He shook his head and then set off along the trail away from the water. It was probably only a kid on a lark, but he should check the situation out. Arcadia Heights might be far removed from the city, but crime had a way of finding the innocent everywhere. With four women living next door, it would be neighborly to scout the area.

Right. And someone would sell him a rosebush to plant in the Alaskan tundra.

Within minutes he reached the perimeter of the McCall yard. A figure stepped into the golden pool of light thrown by the porch light. Nora. What had she been doing in the woods?

Connor started to call out but stopped. What would they have to talk about? Discussing business with an attractive woman at nine o'clock on a Saturday night would be grim. The cold snap of the air and the hushed silence of the woods called for cuddling by the lake, not business.

His mouth curved in self-mockery. Given Nora's "I'm attorney, you client" attitude she'd worn this afternoon, he had a snowflake's chance in hell of getting close to her. He turned.

"Who's out there?" Nora's voice wobbled and then firmed.

Damn. He had forgotten to switch off his flashlight. Connor sighed and called out. "It's just me, Nora."

"Connor?" She came to the porch's edge.

He crossed the yard and halted at the base of the steps. "I was taking a walk in the woods and heard a sound. I was checking it out when I saw you."

"Oh." Nora wrapped her arms around her middle. "Well, thanks."

"You're welcome."

"Abby likes to wander in the woods. I hope that won't disturb you."

Memories of another teenage girl in the forest ran through his mind. He braced his foot on the lower step while Bran took off to explore. "Like mother, like daughter."

A faint smile lit her face, as if a lamp glowed deep within her. "No, Abby is much more adventurous than I was. Sweeter. Stronger." Nora's eyes were smoky crystals, luminous with a mother's pride.

A thorny mix of regret and envy twisted within him, scraping him raw. It was if he was looking at a scrapbook of his life and finding empty pages. Where there should be pictures of a family, there were none. His father had been killed in a car accident before he was born, and his mother had wished he'd never been born. What would it be like to share a child with Nora?

Connor shoveled his fingers through his hair. Nora already had a child, and Abby wasn't his. He hadn't returned to Arcadia Heights to start over; he was here to pay off an old debt.

It was sure going to be hard to keep telling himself that lie whenever he was in Nora's presence. The warm porch light drew interesting shadows on her features, especially that one tempting hollow along her collarbone left exposed by her jacket.

He had risked much to face his past so that he could move forward. What was one more gamble?

He advanced a step and indicated the stand of trees between their homes. "You appear to have conquered your night fears."

Nora's smile slipped. "Appearances are what I do best." She backed away.

The cryptic remark irked him. Her movement away from him irked him more. "Nora, wait." He bolted up the remaining steps.

She lifted her chin with the kind of hauteur designed to keep a man at twenty paces. "What is it?"

A splash from the flashlight betrayed her nervousness. The wind reached into the porch's shelter and teased loose a few strands of her hair. He lifted his hand and touched the silken tendrils. Her hair was as cool and soft as he remembered it. Would her skin feel the same?

He traced his fingertips along the elegant line of her jaw, feeling her tremble. She pulled her head away from his touch, but he captured her chin and lifted her face to his. Was it just wishful thinking, or was it desire he now saw darkening her eyes? There was only one way to find out. He lowered his head and covered her mouth with his.

He had meant the kiss to be a mere brush of the lips, but he couldn't help himself. He lingered, tasting the sweetness of her mouth. Then, when she softened against him and sighed, he deepened the kiss.

And unleashed a pulsing urgency inside him to make Nora his again. He slid a hand around her waist and jerked her against him, hard.

In an instant Nora's body went from soft to brittle. She wrenched away. Her kiss-reddened lips quivered briefly before she pressed them together.

Connor silently cursed himself. He treated his plants with more care than he had handled her, especially after her panic this afternoon. With a tremendous effort, he yanked a leash around his careening need.

"Sorry, Nora. I didn't mean to be so intense."

She crossed her arms over her breasts. Her protective gesture drove a heavy fist of guilt into his stomach. He steeled himself for the stinging rebuke he deserved.

"It's okay."

Her words were so low he wasn't sure he heard them. "What?"

She rubbed her arms as if chilled. His blood was still so hot he felt as if steam must be rolling off him. She looked him square in the eye.

"Connor, I'm a woman, not the teenager you remember." She said softly, almost to herself, "I'm not sure I was ever that teenager." She gave a shrug. "I know all too well about physical needs and desires."

For some reason her comment didn't sit well with him. He didn't like the idea that Nora had explored passion with another man.

That's all in the past, he reminded himself.

"But I'm not interested in digging up an old affair that's been long dead for both of us. For the time you're here, Connor, it's best if we keep matters on a professional level." She reached behind her, opened the door and slipped inside. "Good night."

Ha. That's what she thought. Before she could shut the door, he crossed the landing and planted his foot on the threshold. He brought his face close to her startled one. "You're mistaken on two counts."

She moistened her lips.

Good. He had her attention. He leaned forward until his breath stirred her hair. "One, I'm not here for a visit. I'm here to start a business. Two—" he dipped his head until his mouth hovered a kiss away "—if what we shared moments ago was blighted desire, you've been in hibernation far too long. I'll just have to cultivate you."

Enjoying her indignant gasp, Connor allowed himself the pleasure of nipping her lower lip. He smiled slowly as her gasp turned into a moan. He removed his foot from the doorway, turned and went down the steps.

* * *

Why? Why had he left her?

Nora started awake with the question on her lips, lips that still tasted Connor's soul-searing kiss. Dim light crept across the bedroom floor. She glanced at the clock on the stand. Six-fifteen.

She threw back the twisted comforter and rose. Even the cool dawn before her couldn't chill the memories of last night. She rubbed her hands over her arms. No question about it. She'd had a close call.

His passion as a man was something she'd never experienced, never realized existed. Such heat and hunger, such tantalizing pleasure. Relentless hot waves had drawn her into the dark tide of his possession until she had practically drowned in him. Only the sudden press of his aroused body had brought her to her senses before it'd been too late.

She now knew what her mother had meant.

Staring sightlessly out the window, Nora no longer saw the backyard. Instead, she saw the dingy interior of a squalid apartment.

"Please, Mom, don't go out tonight." She thrust her thin eight-year-old body in front of the door.

Tess, heavily perfumed, pushed her aside. Pausing in the opened doorway, she leaned close to Nora and whispered, "You'll understand when you're older, kid. The only time I can forget is when I'm lost in a man." Then she had left, leaving Nora to cope with her sick sister.

Lost in a man. Nora closed her eyes and pressed her throbbing temple against the chilled glass. Was she no better than her mother? All Connor had to do was touch her, and she turned into putty.

Yet, on some deep level, it didn't feel wrong. Only Connor had ever felt right to her.

She thumped her head lightly against the pane and then straightened. Since there was no going back to sleep this Sunday, she could always work on her brief until the others awoke. Anything to keep her troubling thoughts of Connor at bay. She crossed to the door and went into the hallway.

All was silent, but her mind found no peace in the stillness. Compelled, she walked to her daughter's bedroom and carefully turned the knob. She'd just look in, reassure herself that Abby was all right.

Nora stepped inside.

Abby's bed was empty.

The kitchen's overhead light glared harshly in the predawn hour, its naked bulb consistent with the rest of the stark surroundings. As Connor tugged on his work boots, he morosely surveyed the room. The once-white linoleum was gray with age and grime. The sooty wood of the cabinets bore testament to years of cooking with grease. Somewhere under the smoke-crusted surface Connor thought oak paneling might exist. The pea-green Formica countertops were chipped and knife-scarred.

Sighing, Connor stood and crossed to the counter by the rusted steel sink where his coffeemaker sat—a gleaming high-tech alien amidst the kitchen relics—and poured himself a mug. He took a bracing swallow, and the liquid scalded his tongue. He inhaled and exhaled deeply before taking another gulp.

Connor eased his hip against the sink and looked out the curtained window. In the misty light he could see the shadowy outlines of the barn and sheds. Bran, out for his morning constitutional, was circling the yard. Beyond the buildings, dark ripples of fields edged the black forest on the left side.

This was all his now. The only home he'd ever known.

He shook his head. "Ed, you old coot. What were you thinking when you left me this place?" The room was silent. The farmer's presence would be felt outside in his beloved fields and gardens.

Connor contemplated the awakening vista. In its shadows he could still see the big red-haired man with a weathered voice. Throwing a lifeline to a lonely twelve-year-old boy. Connor's fingers tightened around the mug.

Connor had been huddled by the lake on a cold blustery Christmas when Ed had found him. Sheila Devlin had been making the rounds of her parishioners, and she hadn't wanted her son with her. Ed had taken one long look at Connor's eyes, gritty from repressed tears, and without comment, had brought him back to his kitchen for a cup of hot chocolate. The farmer had then stood in this very spot and given him something no one else had given him—a chance. "Son, if you're going to be skulking around all the time, I might as well put you to work."

True to his word, the old man had put him to work, from morning to night. There had been no more time to think of ways to rile his mother to gain attention. Connor had been too busy learning how to coax life out of the seeds he planted in the fields. While his mother charmed her parishioners, Ed had shown Connor the joy of babying a rosebud into a spectacular blossom.

Connor sipped his coffee. He thought about the cryptic remark in Ed's will that the lawyer had read to him over the phone.

"It's time for the boy to come home."

Well, for once Ed was wrong. Connor would establish his newest landscaping franchise, fulfill Ed's last request, rub the collective nose of Arcadia Heights in Primal Rose's success and then return to Florida. At the same time, he'd purge himself of the persistent memories of young love.

Connor turned away, but images of the past held him captive. Instead of the battered shell of a kitchen, he could see a glistening blue-and-white-tile floor, rich wood cabinets with brass fittings, federal-blue counters and blue-and-white-sprigged wallpaper. Sheer curtains letting in the dawn's early glow. The sumptuous scent of coffee mingling with frying bacon. And standing at the glossy white stove, stood a tall slender woman, her long black hair pulled carelessly back into a ponytail.

Nora McCall. His boyish dream should have dulled over the years. Instead, it remained vivid and full-blown.

He blinked, and the image blurred, then disappeared. The vision had been so real that the smell of the bacon still lingered. He could make it a reality. If he ripped out the cabinetry today and headed over to the nearest building-supply store to check out materials...

Connor took a step and stopped. What was he thinking? Building a home? He rubbed his face.

He had a place. This house was only a fixer-upper for showcase purposes. He was picking the fruit off the tree before he had even planted the seed. Time to get his butt in gear and outside. The first greenhouse was going up tomorrow.

Connor shrugged into his jacket and picked up the

bag by the kitchen door. He then went out to the porch and across the yard and stopped in front of one of the sheds slated for destruction. Reaching for the door handle, he froze. There was a rustling noise and then a soft oath.

"Doggone it! I'm just trying to help you. I've got to get you out of here before he comes."

Connor pulled open the door and stepped inside. He stood still, letting his eyes adjust to the dark interior. The musty air assailed his nose; he stifled a sneeze. He swung his head toward the source of another muttered oath. He blinked.

In the corner, a major face-off was in progress: a very disheveled Abby was sucking on her knuckle while she exchanged glares with a hissing orange-striped cat. Gingerly Abby stuck out her hand toward one of the small grunting balls of fur crawling over the moldy straw. With a quick swipe the cat nailed her. Yipping, Abby snatched her hand back and sucked on it again.

"You don't understand. This place's going to be toast soon. I've got to get the kittens to safety before the bad man finds you."

"Does your mother know you talk like that?" Connor asked gently from behind her.

Abby screeched and fell backward, sprawling on the floor. Connor stood over her and folded his arms. "Since I'm obviously the 'bad man,' what do you think I'll be doing with the kittens?"

The girl propped herself on her elbows and blew a wayward curl out of her face. The defiant tilt of her chin was just like her mother's. An unidentifiable emotion twisted in Connor at seeing the identical spirit in her daughter.

"You'll toss them in the lake and drown them."

Connor took a half step back, staggered by the unexpected blow. How could this child think he would do something so heinous? What kind of man did she think he was? Who had said such things about him to her?

Through his churning thoughts, a name floated to the surface. Nora.

Anger flared within him. Did Nora hate him so much that she filled her daughter's ears with lies? He bit back a curse and carefully asked, "Where would you get such a notion? From your mother?"

Even in the dim light he could see Abby's face redden. She shook her head and tried to get up. He reached out and tugged the girl to her feet. She hung her head and jammed her hands into her front jeans pockets. "No, sir."

Relief rippled through him. "Who, then?"

She shrugged. "No one. I just thought…"

He cupped her chin, lifting her face for his inspection. "You thought what, Abby?" He kept his voice gentle.

"People were talking about you at the game yesterday. I overheard Mr. Ames call you a hellion, quick with your fists. There's a kid in my class, Chuck Partridge. He's mean. Always getting into trouble in class, picking on kids smaller than him." Her lower lip trembled.

"Let me guess. He also torments animals."

She nodded. "When Mom said at dinner last night you were going to be tearing down the old sheds today, I panicked. I come here all the time to…well, I just come. Mr. Miller never minded. That's how I knew 'bout the stray cat with her kittens. I was going to move them before you found the litter.''

"Because you figured if I was a bad apple, I might hurt them like Chuck would.''

She shook her head, her eyes shimmering in the shadows. "Pretty stupid, huh?''

He dropped his hand. "It won't be the first time someone has jumped to the wrong conclusion about me.''

Abby took a shuddering breath. "That's what Mr. Millman said.''

Connor frowned. "Lawrence Millman?''

"No.'' A strange look crossed her face. "His son, David. He's been taking Mom out to dinner.''

Before Connor could stew over her comment, Abby gasped, "You're feeding the cat!''

The evidence of his good intentions lay on the floor: a five-pound bag of seafood-flavor cat food. Connor tucked his hands in his jacket pockets and shrugged uncomfortably. "The last time I checked, it wasn't a crime to feed cats.'' The corner of his mouth kicked up. "Though my dog, Bran, would beg to differ with me.''

The girl's smile, so much like her mother's, touched a cord deep within him. How he had loved to say outrageous things to bring a blush to Nora's face. How strange that he wanted nothing more of this moment than to make her child like him. To hide his discomfort, Connor knelt down and took a plastic scoop out of the cat-food bag. Abby crouched down beside him and held the sack's edges.

Her hands. So slight and delicate with youth, yet sculpted with the promise of strength. If he could go back and remake the past, those hands waiting for him could have, would have, belonged to his own daughter, his child with Nora.

Connor ruthlessly squelched the thought and jammed the scoop into the dry food. He couldn't go back. Decisions had been made, actions taken, and his and Nora's lives had followed their separate paths. All he could do now was follow a different course and see where it took him.

He grabbed the bowl he kept in the shed and dumped the food into it. The mama cat immediately shook off her squeaking kittens and came to him. "Good morning, girl." Connor scratched the animal behind her ears and was rewarded with a throaty purr. Smaller fingers brushed his as they joined in stroking the cat's head.

"I call her Pumpkin," Abby said, "because she's orange and plump and such a sweetie."

He glanced down at Abby's upturned face. She beamed, her wonderful blue eyes sparkling. His heart lurched and was lost to the child. Connor nodded. "Well, then, Pumpkin she is." He gave the cat one last stroke under the chin and stood.

Abby rose and looked up at him, her brows slightly furrowed. "Uh, Mr. Devlin…"

"Connor's my name."

She nodded. "Connor. I'm sorry for what I said earlier."

Connor dared to lay his hand briefly on her shoulder. "Forget it."

She nodded. He turned and exited the shed. The sun hung low in the eastern horizon, casting a reddish glow to the frost shrouded landscape. Abby stood beside him, a look of sheer delight on her face. "I love this farm," she whispered. "I never get tired of looking at the land. It constantly changes. Right now the light's all rose and gold.''

She bit her lower lip and shot him an embarrassed glance from under lowered lashes. ''Don't tell anyone I said that.''

Casually Connor dropped an arm around her stiff shoulders. ''I won't. I feel the same way myself. Whenever I had a problem as a kid, I would come here. Even if I never found the answer, I would find life wasn't as bad as I thought it was. That I could handle the trouble.''

He tightened his hold protectively when Abby flashed him a look of sheer relief. ''That's it. That's how I feel!''

It looked like Ed Miller had touched another life. ''Do you want to help me clear some land? I can tell you what I'm planning to do.''

Abby shrugged, but her eyes glowed with excitement. ''Sure. If you have the time.''

He waggled his eyebrows. ''I always have time to tell a beautiful girl my grandiose plans.'' Abby rewarded him with another rolling of her eyes. Classic McCall.

He gestured. ''Along this stretch by the driveway will be a flower-lined pergola. I'm going to convert the barn into a gardening store with books, tools, seeds and plants.'' With Abby in tow, he continued to where the dilapidated toolshed stood. ''This goes, and in its place I'll construct a country gallery, showcasing local crafts, including—'' he grinned ''—hand-thrown pottery. Most of the remaining sheds will have to be torn down.'' At her distressed look, he hurried to reassure her. ''But not the one Pumpkin's in. At least not until we find homes for her kittens.''

Abby's face broke out into a dazzling smile, its radiance overpowering. His heart more than belonged to the girl, Connor thought ruefully as he ran his hand over his chest. Hell, Nora and he might be at eternal odds, but Abby had his protection for life.

The fallen leaves crackled under Nora's feet as she hurried along the path that snaked through the forest. With autumn ending, the maple, oak and ash trees were in the process of closing up shop. Bare branches outnumbered those with leaves, and the dark winter firs patiently awaited their turn to shine.

A thorough search of the house and shop had yielded no sign of Abby. There was only one place left to search before she pulled the panic lever—the Miller farm.

From the moment she had first shared the silent wonder of the copse with her daughter, Abby had been drawn to the farm abutting their property. Fortunately Ed Miller had never minded her wayward child's intrusion and her endless questions.

That all had to change now. With Connor being the new owner, she had to make Abby understand she couldn't just traipse over there anymore. Nora shivered and drew her fleece jacket tighter. Many things were going to change now.

Reaching the other side of the forest, Nora paused. Effervescent laughter broke the early-morning quiet, followed by a low rough chuckle. Nora crossed the yard to the other side of the house.

Abby stood splay-legged, picking up rocks and tossing them in a pile. Her face was flushed under the bill of her prized *Star Wars* baseball cap. Clad in only a white T-shirt and faded torn jeans, Connor worked beside the girl, handling the larger stones and debris. Connor's enormous black dog, on a return trip from the mound, paused expectantly by Abby and received her pat on his head.

Nora's heart lurched painfully, so painfully that she placed her hand over her chest to keep it contained. They fit together, her daughter and the man who was her father. They shared eyes as blue as the crystal autumn sky, a ready smile and a joyful expression from working the land.

If she'd had any doubt about telling them the truth, it was swept away forever by seeing them together. If only Connor hadn't left her, they would have been a family. Longing for what might have been pierced her like a thorn.

Where was her pride?

He had left her. Whatever they had shared was dead and buried. Forget what happened last night, forget his kiss. All that mattered was Abby.

Nora lifted her chin. Her voice came out harsh and sharp with guilt. "Abigail McCall! I've been looking for you everywhere. You had me worried sick!"

Chagrin chased away the happiness on her daughter's face. She jammed her grimy hands in the pockets of her jacket. "I'm sorry, Mom."

Wiping his hands on the front of his jeans, Connor thoughtfully studied Nora's face. To Nora's surprise he turned to Abby and quietly asked, "You didn't tell your mother where you were?"

Abby studied her feet and shook her head.

"Didn't you think she'd be worried?"

Another shake of the head, this time accompanied by a shrug.

He placed a finger under their daughter's chin, forcing her contrite eyes to meet his. "Abby, any time you want to come here, that's fine by me."

Nora's lips thinned with displeasure. She was going to have to play bad cop. Her protest died on her lips as Connor continued, "But I won't allow you to come unless you tell your mom where you are, every single time. Do we have an understanding?"

Abby nodded and then flashed a tentative smile. "Yes, Connor." He continued to look at her sternly. Her smile faded.

"Your mother has enough to worry about. She doesn't need you adding to her burdens."

Despite the warmth his unexpected support had fanned in her, Nora stepped forward when she saw her daughter's shoulders droop.

Connor chucked Abby on the chin, then circled her shoulders, hugging her. "Enough of the lecture. Why don't you get us a drink of water while I convince your mom to help with the cleanup?"

Two pairs of identical blue eyes looked at Nora expectantly. A pang of longing curled around her heart and squeezed painfully. If only, Nora thought. If only things had been different, this would have been hers, every day. But it wasn't. She couldn't go back, only forward.

With a bounce in her step, Abby set off for the house.

"Nora?" Looking puzzled, Connor closed the distance between them. "Are you all right?"

He smelled of soil and sweat. Pure male. This time the pang shot to her core. She swayed slightly and closed her eyes against the painful tingle of sensations awakened by last night's kiss.

He gripped her, his voice low, concerned. "Hey,

what's wrong? The kid's fine. She didn't think, that's all.''

Yes, she did—or rather, Nora did—and that was the problem. She remembered his touch, his taste, his texture. She remembered his heat.

She drew a deep breath and forced herself to meet his intent gaze. "I'm fine." Her attempt at a smile, though, failed miserably.

Something flared and smoldered in Connor's eyes. He reached up and trailed the side of his finger down her cheek. Her skin warmed beneath his touch. Desire coursed like liquid fire through her body. His gaze fell to her throat where she knew her pulse throbbed, exposing her reaction to him. He stepped back.

"Are you sure?"

Bemused, Nora wondered what she was supposed to be sure about. She couldn't think, not when he stood so close his warm breath caressed her face. Over the thundering heartbeat in her ears, she heard the porch door slam.

The sound chilled her rampant emotions. What on earth was wrong with her? Where was that willpower she prided herself on?

Determinedly Nora broke eye contact with Connor. "I'm fine." She stepped away from him. "I believe the question is whether I'll help with the cleanup detail. Where do I start?"

She ignored Connor's amused chuckle as she sauntered over to the cleared tract.

Chapter Four

Tuesday night Nora stopped short of slamming the portable phone down. "Of all the small-minded..."

"Something wrong?" Eve didn't look away from the Cincinnati Bengals football game she had taped Sunday.

"That was Abby's art teacher. Their new class project is to copy an old master."

"So?" Eve munched a handful of buttered popcorn.

"So Abby wanted to do a figurine but was told she couldn't. I phoned to find out why." Recalling the teacher's snippy condescending tone made Nora's jaw tense. "According to Mrs. Barnsworth, the purpose of the assignment is quote 'to study and emulate a famous painter—only' unquote."

Eve crunched thoughtfully and swallowed. "Ever hear of Michelangelo?"

Nora snatched a handful of popcorn, neatly avoiding her sister's defensive swipe. "Of course."

"He's a painter—" Eve flicked a kernel at her "—and a sculptor."

Nora paused in polishing off her popcorn and grinned. "So if Abby copies him, she could do a sketch of the work and then the actual figurine."

"Hard to top *David*," Eve agreed as she turned back to the TV. "From the waist up, of course."

"Absolutely. Thanks." Nora left the family room, crossed the hallway and went up the stairs. Quietly she entered her daughter's bedroom. Only the dark crown of Abby's head could be seen over the edge of the pink comforter.

Nora folded the edge of the comforter and plucked a teen magazine that was spread open on the bed. "Sorry," she told Ricky Martin's beaming face. "You'll have to enthrall my daughter another time." She placed the magazine on the nightstand and paused before turning out the lamp. Reaching down, she brushed a wayward curl from Abby's sleep-flushed cheek.

"Mom? What's a pergola?" Abby barely opened her eyes.

"What, honey?"

"A pergola." Abby turned onto her back. "Connor's building one, and I forgot to ask him what it was."

Nora arched a brow. "After playing twenty questions Sunday, you actually forgot to ask one?" Abby had peppered Connor until sundown, but he had patiently answered every question.

"Oh, Mom." Abby yawned and stretched.

Nora sat on the edge of the bed. "A pergola is an arbor with latticework, usually vine-covered."

"Mmm. That will be pretty." Abby played with the edge of the comforter. "I had fun Sunday, you know, with the three of us working together."

"I did, too, sweetheart." It had been fun, Nora realized. Abby's endless chatter had broken the initial awkward silence between her and Connor. After that, the three of them had fallen into an easy camaraderie.

Abby giggled. "I thought you were going to have a cow when Connor suggested you make lunch."

Nora dryly said, "'Ordered' is more like it."

Her daughter grinned. "Sorry I spilled the beans about your cooking."

Recalling Connor's reaction to Abby's pronouncement that her mother didn't have a clue in the kitchen, Nora tried to suppress her smile. The man had scowled, then muttered under his breath some absurd comment about planting seeds before they germinated. Despite his grousing, Connor had whipped up soul-satisfying ham and Swiss sandwiches along with hot chocolate.

"But I managed to boil the water for the cocoa," Nora bragged. "No small task with that ancient ruin of a stove."

Abby yawned. "Sure, Mom."

She caressed her daughter's cheek. "Shut-eye time for you. You have early soccer practice tomorrow." She rose. "Good night, hon." She reached for the lamp pull.

"Mom?"

"What?" She looked down and found her daughter studying her somberly.

"Do you like Connor?"

Her heart stuttered. "Why?"

"I think he likes you."

Nora rubbed her damp palms along her legs. "Of course he does, honey. After all, we grew up together."

Abby chewed her lower lip. "I don't know about that, Mom. He looks at you like the men do in those coffee commercials. You know, where the man makes up excuses to borrow a cup of coffee from his beautiful neighbor. Like he can't help it?"

Out of the mouths of babes, Nora thought as she stood, flabbergasted. She swallowed and forced a casual tone. "How would you feel if he were interested?"

Concerned, Nora sat down and cupped her daughter's chin. The turmoil she saw in her child's gaze stunned her. It was as if she were that age again, looking into a mirror and seeing the too-old expression in her own eyes. "Abby?"

The confession was a whisper, as if the burden of the admission was all its bearer could handle. "I'm afraid."

"Afraid of what, sweetheart?" Nora wrapped her arms around Abby and drew the small resistant body against hers.

"What if my father comes back and doesn't like me?"

Nora's hand trembled as she smoothed the soft waves of Abby's hair. "Whatever gave you that notion?"

Abby's shoulders jerked. "Some kids."

"Someone's been teasing you?" Nora's spine stiffened.

Another hitch. "Yes, at school."

"About?"

A muffled sniffle. "My father left you because he didn't want me."

"That's ridiculous." Nora closed her eyes. "Abby, I've told you. We were too young to take on the responsibility of being a family."

"But *you* didn't put me up for adoption."

Despite all her terror during the months of her pregnancy, despite all the pressure from Pastor Devlin during the secret counseling sessions, giving up her child had never been a consideration. She pressed a kiss to Abby's temple. "No. I couldn't give up the light of my life."

"Sometimes, I'm afraid I'm lost."

Bewildered, she gathered Abby closer. "You're right here, honey. You're right here with me, Eve and Christina."

Abby wrenched herself free. Anger stained her cheeks. "You don't understand," she accused. "I don't know who my father is since you won't ever tell me because of some stupid promise you made."

"But knowing who he is has never mattered. We've always had each other."

"But, Mom—" Abby's eyes revealed a dangerous undercurrent "—part of me is missing, the part that belongs to my father."

Nora kept her voice light. "You are your own person, and a pretty terrific person at that."

Abby flopped down and turned her back. "I knew you wouldn't understand. Go away."

Nora hesitated and then rose. "All right. We'll discuss this more later. Good night, sweetheart. I love you."

"Umph" was Abby's only response.

Nora turned off the light and left the room. Numb, she walked along the hall into the kitchen.

Her gaze lit on the refrigerator, which was covered with photographs. She stepped closer and studied a faded Polaroid of the McCall sisters and Aunt Abigail, taken shortly after their arrival in Arcadia Heights.

Solemn grey eyes stared back at her, the eyes of a girl old beyond her years, who had never known the carefree joy of being a child, of having the love of her parents.

She heard her mother's taunting voice, *"Like mother, like daughter."*

"No!" Nora pressed the back of her hand to her mouth to choke back any further cry. She rested her forehead against the cold refrigerator door. How could she have been so blind?

She was forging the same path for Abby as Tess had for her. Condemning her to a fatherless existence, never knowing to whom she belonged.

Was she too late to stop any more harm from being done?

"Ed," Connor addressed the plain gravestone, "what have you gotten me into?"

Ed had chosen his and his wife's final resting place well. They were buried on a knoll overlooking the lake they had loved so much. An arbor of maples shielded them from the bite of the winter wind and the unrelenting heat of the summer sun.

When he was a teenager, Connor had found a battered wrought-iron bench, which he had sanded, painted and hauled to this spot, allowing Ed to visit with his wife every night after his chores were done.

Connor sat on the bench now, watching the black

ripples of the lake play catch with the pale moonbeams. This Tuesday night, the moonlight was winning, sparkling with the pride of victory as it skimmed across the surface.

But no truths could be divined by staring at the lake tonight; it was as dark as his own thoughts.

What was he doing here? When he had gotten the phone call about Ed's death and the inheritance of the farm, his plan had been simple. Return to Arcadia Heights, build the first botanical garden, eradicate the ghosts from his past and return to Florida.

Ha. Connor picked up a stone and hurled it into the lake. Its soft *plop* was the only sound in the night. He thought he had sweated out all the anger, all the indignation, all the hurt inflicted by his mother and the town. He thought he had buried his youthful dreams of a loving family in the sandy soil of Florida.

But now his plan to thumb his nose at the town was being shot to hell by one irrefutable fact: he still had feelings for Nora.

He scowled at the twilight vista before him. He had been certain that if they resumed their affair, they both would find that its shelf life had expired. But the mind-numbing kiss on Saturday night had smashed that illusion. As a teenager Nora had been enticing; as a woman she was mesmerizing.

He picked up another stone and hurled it.

There was the town's reaction to consider, as well. Sheila Devlin hadn't been the mother he needed, but he hadn't been the son she had wanted. It shouldn't matter to him what the community thought, but it did. The standoffish attitude he had experienced left a need in him…but for what? Acceptance?

But how could he change their opinion without risking Sheila's retribution? He glanced over at the tombstone. "You once told me Mom couldn't help herself and I shouldn't fight what I couldn't change, just as a farmer shouldn't rage against the weather. You told me I was only responsible for what I made of myself. But, Ed—" Connor picked up yet another stone "—how does an outcast seed put down roots in ruined soil?"

No answer.

Time for a reality check, he admonished himself. Nothing could be done about the town's opinion. He wasn't here to stay, so there was no point even thinking about it.

A burst of lake water suddenly sprayed his face. Connor sighed, wiped his forehead and rubbed Bran's dripping head. "You big lug," he scolded. "Can't you enjoy your swim without sharing it?" In response, the dog pressed its wet body against Connor's leg. He laughed and pushed Bran away. "Listen, pal, I'm not equipped with a built-in fur coat."

Connor rose and made his way along the winding path back to the house. His pulse kicked up when he saw a silhouette inside the translucent walls of the newly erected conservatory. He wasn't expecting anyone. He quickened his step and yanked open the door.

The evening sky was clear, with a faint sprinkling of stars. The moon was only a sliver, its pale light a flicker seen through the swaying treetops.

Nora hurried along the path through the forest. She had planned to drive to Connor's, but when she had gone outside, the dark trees had summoned her. The trees along the path seemed to whisper their disapproval. From time to time Nora spotted the red-eye glints of animals in the brush. Her jury, she thought half hysterically.

At a bend in the path, she halted. Spotlighted in the broad beam of her flashlight was a great horned owl perched on an overhanging branch. The stately bird scrutinized her. Nora glared back. "Forget it. I'm not condemned—yet."

The owl's sage eyes twinkled. With a lift of its huge wings, the bird heaved itself off the branch and disappeared into the night. Nora continued on.

When she reached the *Y,* she turned right and headed to the Miller farmstead. At the clearing, she caught her breath as she saw a small pearly building with a low-pitched roof. Through the frosted panes she could see the outline of plant rows. The incubator of life drew her inside.

It was like entering a tropical paradise. She felt as if she was on a pilgrimage, leaving behind autumn and its prophecy of death to embark into life's womb with its promise of rebirth. The air smelled of earth and water and heat. Overhead, a pipe hissed. Nora watched a fine spray of water douse a row of plants.

This was pure Connor, she realized. This was what Connor had become.

She wandered in deeper to a pair of workbenches. On one were tied bundles of pruned rosebushes. Stark and thorny, they showed no hint of life. Under Connor's touch, they would flourish. The neat rows of healthy plants surrounding her bore testament to his skill.

Remembering his talented hands, she shivered. She ran a finger over a green leaf of a potted rose placed next to the closest bench.

Nora's determination to confront Connor and tell

him about Abby was melting away, drop by drop. Yet, guilt still snapped at her, dogging her every thought.

Her gaze fell on the potted rosebush, its deep-red buds hinting at the beauty to come.

So much promise.

Yet, with its hidden thorns, so much danger.

Was Connor like that? Capable of beauty yet violence? Rumors of a fight Monday afternoon between Connor and a construction worker had provided a savory stew for the town to feed on. If true, the image was contradictory to the image of Connor talking with Abby.

And then there was *that* kiss.

But a night and day of pleasant company did not equal a torrid affair. A commitment to build a business didn't mean a commitment to a relationship with her, let alone to a lifetime of fatherhood. She must keep her association with Connor on a professional level.

She must. She needed a clear head in order to assess what was best for Abby. Her daughter must never suffer the hellish nightmare of rejection and abandonment.

Connor's eminent return to Florida didn't mean he could not be a long-distance father. After all, many parents maintained contact with their children while living in different states.

Oh, God, could she entrust her daughter to him?

"I didn't expect you tonight."

"Oh!" Nora spun around, her heart bounding into her throat.

Despite the strong overhead lighting, Connor was, well, magnificent. The black jeans and turtleneck he wore under his unzipped leather jacket only emphasized his sleek masculine power. Her fingers longed to touch his windblown hair...

No. She mustn't think like that. She tried to circle around him, but he blocked her path.

His dimple flashed. "One would almost think you're afraid of being alone with me."

And one would think right, but she wasn't about to let him know it. "Don't flatter yourself, Devlin. I was merely trying to see what color the roses are on the bush behind you."

His grin broadened, but he stepped aside with a sweep of his hand. She pretended to study the slightly unfurled bud, then pretense transformed into delight. "It's like a fireball wrapped in silver tissue!"

Surprise lit Connor's eyes, and his cocky smile slipped. He knelt beside her and ran a knuckle gently along the fluted edges of the rose. "This is a Milestone. It's red with a silvery reverse. When it's in full bloom, the color will become more of a coral-pink."

Nora bent over, sniffed and frowned. "I don't smell anything."

Connor nodded, his head so near she could see the rich weave of brown, red and gold in his hair.

"Milestones have only a slight fragrance. Something I'm working on." Connor rose abruptly.

Puzzled by the flush staining his cheeks, she straightened. "Is something wrong?"

"Not a thing." He moved to the bench.

She followed. "You said you were working on something. Are you breeding roses yourself?"

He shot her an amused glance. "You don't breed plants. The word is *cultivate*." He picked up a pair of shears, tested his grip, winced and then laid it down again.

"Oh." Nora absorbed the intriguing bit of information as she braced her hip against the table. His interests went beyond growing. He created plant life. This was a deep layer to Connor that she hadn't expected to uncover. "Do you have any here?"

He pulled out a pocketknife and flicked out a blade. "Do I have what here?"

She suppressed a sigh. Connor always turned taciturn when he didn't want to expose himself to ridicule. "Roses you've cultivated." It would be the right moment to tell him the truth, she decided.

He hitched one shoulder.

Nora took the gesture for a yes. "May I see them?" When he showed her the flowers, she would tell him about another life—a very precious human one—that he had created.

He slashed through the heavy twine and winced again. He then set down the knife and rubbed his hand.

Alarmed, she slid closer. "Did you cut yourself?"

"Nope. Bruised them yesterday. They're just stiffer than heck."

The fight. When she had asked their friend Nate Roberts if it was true, Nate had only chuckled and said that Connor had taken up the old-fashioned sport of caber tossing. She wet her lips. "I heard you had a disagreement with a worker."

His devil-may-care mask in place, Connor turned to face her. "Is that lawyer-speak for a fight? If it is, then the answer is yes. Like all the other people trapped in this burg, the man had a big mouth and a nose a mile too long."

Trapped. His icy words pelted her. He still felt the same about his hometown. How could she set the cage over him now? If he lashed out, he could wound Abby for life.

She straightened. "Well, it's late, and you look like you're busy."

Despite his calm demeanor, she could feel the suppressed energy inside him. He reached out and snared her elbow. "What's the matter, Nora? Do you think I beat up the man deliberately?" He tugged her closer. "That I'm the bad apple my mother always harped about?" Resentment sizzled in his eyes.

Nora cast a desperate glance around her. Her gaze rested on the bench behind Connor and an escape plan formed in her mind. She relaxed, allowing herself to be drawn to him. She rested her hands lightly on his chest before tilting her head so she could challenge his stare.

"No," she replied calmly.

Surprise flitted across his face. "No?"

"No, I don't think you're a scourge of the earth. I never did." She measured the distance behind them and leaned toward the hard contours of his body. Despite herself, a thrill whipped through her. She should fear him. The raw power of him could overwhelm her, destroy her control. "My worry was you would lose sight of yourself in a perverse compulsion to prove that everyone's opinion of you was right."

His grip loosened. "Nora." He bent his head.

It was now or never. Once he kissed her, she would be a goner. She nudged him into the branch of thorns hanging over the table.

"Ow!" Connor let go of her and whipped around. His hand rubbed his back. "That hurt."

Nora broke for the door. She never made it.

He grabbed her elbow and hauled her back to him. The scowl on his face could have started a fire. "Hey! What's going on here? You want me, I want you." To prove his point, he cupped her buttocks and pressed her against his arousal.

Shock pulsed through her, followed by need that was as sharp as it was sweet. Her surroundings went into a slow spin as Connor nipped her earlobe. There was something she needed to tell him, but how could she think while his touch was setting her blood on fire?

"If you're worrying about your boyfriend David Millman, forget him." His lips skimmed her throat.

David? Why was he talking about David? She couldn't think through the mists of passion swirling in her head.

Connor's hand slid inside her jacket and palmed her breast. "Tonight I'm going to make you forget every man who's ever touched you."

Every man? There had only been him. The implication chilled her as surely as if a northeaster had howled through the greenhouse.

"No!"

Connor was not to be deterred, if the determined glint in his eyes was any indication. He reached for her again. "Honey, what's the problem? We're both free to do what we want."

Her anger burned raw and hot. Heedless of caution, she let it flow. "Yes, just like we did twelve years ago. Only, you got to do what you wanted, leaving me alone to face all the consequences."

Connor ran his fingers through his hair. "What are you talking about?"

Nora called upon all her reserves and drew herself up to face truth's firing squad. "The consequences of unprotected sex."

Connor flushed and rocked back on his heels. "Hell, Nora," he muttered. "I was clean."

"That's not the consequence I was talking about."

He frowned. "Then what are you..." His voice trailed off.

Nora brought her chin up. "I'm referring to the baby I carried for nine months and then raised. Abby, your daughter."

Connor stared in disbelief at the calm woman before him. His life lay in a twisted ruin at his feet, and she had the gall to look as composed as a choir director. Nora McCall was in control of the situation, and he wanted to shake her until he rattled out a reaction, any reaction.

Instead, he jammed his hands into his pockets. He had thought he couldn't be hurt any more. Over the years he had insulated himself from the deprecating remarks and stares of the townspeople and his mother. His heart had become so wrapped in protection that no one should have been able to rip through it to get to his core.

He was wrong. Nora had slashed through to his soul.

He had wanted her all these years. Winning Nora McCall had been the ultimate goal of his homecoming gamble, but her breaking his heart hadn't been part of the plan. He had a daughter, and the defiant woman before him had never told him.

She hadn't thought he was fit to be a father.

Not only had she betrayed him, she had found a way to reject him in a manner from which he might never recover. He wanted to hate her for what she had done to him, to Abby. But he couldn't. She was the mother of his child; she was the woman he had loved.

She was his dream of acceptance and belonging.

"Why, Nora? Tell me why." His voice was hoarse.

She squared her shoulders and angled her chin. "As I recall, you left town and never looked back."

He took a step forward and removed his hands from his pockets, only to clench them at his sides. "I had my reasons, Nora. I did what I thought was best for both of us, at the time." He took another step and watched a muscle jerk in her jaw. "I made sure Ed Miller knew where I was. You knew me, Nora. You knew that I would keep contact with him."

She folded her arms across her chest. "Yes, I knew you did. On occasion I would drop off cake or cookies for him, and he would mention you'd called."

Connor stopped a foot away from her, close enough to touch her, but he couldn't. "Then why didn't you let me know I was a father? Did you think I wouldn't care? That I wouldn't take care of you and the baby?"

Her gaze stony, Nora stood motionless. Anger began to rise in him. Connor wanted to topple her from her pedestal, to smash his fist on top of the table by his side—anything to jar loose her emotions. His temples throbbed, but over the rush of his blood, he could hear Ed Miller's grave voice chastising him. *Learn to channel your emotions, Connor. You punch bags, boy, never people. Don't let your mother's example ruin your life.* Connor curled his fingers into his palms so fiercely that he thought his flesh would rip.

"Did you think I wouldn't love Abby?" he lashed out. "Did you think so little of me?"

Nora staggered back, her hand covering her heart. The overhead light spilled brightly, bringing her face into sharp relief. Her eyes were the dark gray of a winter storm, all turmoil and anguish. "No, Connor. I didn't think that. I thought so little of *myself.*" Her lips quivered and then firmed.

Realizing she wasn't going to say anything more, he glared at her. "That's it? That's all the reason you're going to give me?"

"I don't owe you an explanation—" Nora recrossed her arms "—but I do owe you an apology. I should have told you the truth the moment you returned to town, and for that I'm sorry."

He glanced at a rosebush glowing with pink blooms on the workbench. "This is about your damn loyalty to your sisters, isn't it? No man can ever compete for your affection, can they? Not even the father of your child."

Connor advanced until he had Nora pinned against the bench. He placed his hands on the edge, trapping her. "Well, that's fine with me, Nora."

He lowered his head until he could feel the unsteady rise and fall of her chest, smell her scent of roses, and fear? Her ashen face chilled his anger. A long shudder engulfed her body. Hell, he had frightened her.

Disgusted with himself, Connor held up his hands and stepped away. He had to get out of here and tend to his own wounds.

"I'm giving you until tomorrow afternoon to tell *our* daughter that I'm her father. If you don't, then I'm taking the matter into my own hands and telling her the truth myself." He ignored the glisten of not-quite-suppressed tears in her eyes, turned and issued his parting shot. "You do know how to tell Abby the *truth*, don't you?"

Guilt enveloped Nora's soul like a dank cloak, heavy and pressing. She thought she could endure his recriminations, until he pinned her against the workbench. Fear tore at Nora, choking her and cutting off her plea.

He was going to drag her off to a closet like her mother had done.

Then the trap was sprung. Shaken, Nora drew a deep breath of air. Through the blood roaring in her ears, she heard his final insult about telling Abby the truth. "Don't you dare say something so ugly and then leave me." She reached out and grabbed his arm. He didn't shake her off, but an expression of distaste flickered across his face. How could she make him understand?

"I was wrong to not tell you twelve years ago. I should have known your—" She broke off. She should have realized Sheila Devlin would never have betrayed Nora's confession and ask her son to return home, not when it was against Sheila's interest. "Never mind. I'll concede that point. But I was eighteen, scared and focused on survival." She stood toe-to-toe with him.

"I had to cope with a bloated body and mood swings. One moment I'd be laughing at one of Eve's jokes, and the next crying like there was no tomorrow. That was just the first trimester. In the second trimester, while Cheryl Cavanaugh trotted around in tight sweaters and even tighter pants, I was hiding under shirts the size of tents.

"Then there's the third trimester, when Abby decided to start her soccer practice early, usually at two in the morning. And cravings? I ate up every pound of bacon in the store, which is rather amazing when normally I get sick just smelling the cursed stuff.

"I've sacrificed my life for our child. I'd give my life for her."

Connor reached out, but she batted his hand away. "All my anger came back tenfold with your return to town. I admit it. But tonight I realized how important it might be to Abby to know her father."

She stepped away and folded her arms. "Don't you worry. I'll tell our daughter about you. The question I have is, will you be there when she runs to you? Because I can assure you, she's going to hate me—maybe for the rest of her life—and she's going to need her father. Will you be there?"

Connor's lips thinned, and a dull red stain spread across the sharp planes of his face. "Yes, Nora, I will. Because unlike her mother, she will need me." He spun and stalked out.

The greenhouse door banged shut. Nora whispered to the empty room, "By the way, Connor, I am sorry. So very, very sorry."

Chapter Five

As she stepped into the brisk wind swirling along Maple Street, Nora wondered whether she had been spending too much time at the office. As Charlie Barnett's only associate, she'd thrown herself into the practice, hoping to become partner someday. She worked long hours, drafted important legal documents, handled court appearances in Columbus.

Although Nora saw her daughter off in the morning, she was never home to greet Abby at night. She made all Abby's school events but had to make up the time, spending weekends in the office. Perhaps she should start bringing more files home. She could always work on them after Abby was asleep and she had finished up in the pottery shop.

Or during those long lonely hours Abby would be with her father.

Not wanting to face anyone in Kilning You Softly,

Nora cut through the alley, crossed the yard between the shop and house, and trudged up the back porch steps. She could hear the blast of Faith Hill's singing from the tape player kept on the kitchen windowsill. Abby was definitely home.

Dread closed its clammy fingers around Nora's heart. *I've got to do this.* She gripped the doorknob, took a deep breath and stepped inside.

Abby stood in front of the opened refrigerator door, her hips swaying to the upbeat tune. She tilted a milk carton and drank directly from it.

Nora crossed her arms. "Abigail McCall! We have glasses."

Caught in the act, Abby looked abashed. "But it tastes better straight from the carton, Mom."

Nora studied her daughter. Today Abby was wearing her favorite pair of jeans with her baggy *Star Wars* T-shirt, which matched her baseball cap—last year's birthday presents from Eve. Tendrils of black wavy hair curled around her face.

Abby's brows, now furrowed in puzzlement, framed the clear blue brilliance of her eyes. Her father's eyes. She glanced at the clock and then at Nora. "Mom, is something wrong? You're home so early."

Nora gestured to a chair. "Have a seat, honey. I have to talk to you."

"Eve told you about the party Saturday night, huh?" Abby nibbled at her lower lip as she sat.

Nora forgot her carefully planned opening statement. "What? What about Saturday night?"

"Oh, nothing." Abby looked distressed. She folded her arms and started swinging her leg.

Nora reached over, put her hand on her child's shoulder and squeezed gently. "What party?"

Abby's leg pumped faster. "Joyce Chadwick's having some kids over."

"That's nice. What time?"

"Nine."

"That's a little late even for a Saturday night." Nora spied Abby's telltale swallow. "Joyce's parents are going to be there, aren't they?"

Abby's gaze slipped away to focus on some point over Nora's shoulder. "Uh…I think they're going to a concert in Columbus."

"Let me get this straight." Nora released her hold. "You've been invited to an unchaperoned party?"

Abby jerked her head.

"Are boys invited?"

Abby shrugged. "I guess so."

"No."

"But, Mom!" Abby's gaze whipped back to her mother. "Everyone who's anyone in class is going."

"No, and that's final. Unless I get a call from someone's parents telling me they'll be chaperoning, you're not going."

Abby was in full-scale pout. "It's not as if we're going to do anything wrong. We're just going to hang out and play some music."

In her mind's eye, Nora clearly saw the large bar with its well-stocked liquor cabinet in the Chadwick house. "Abby, I'm sorry. If the party was earlier or if there were adult supervision, you could go, but not under these circumstances."

Rebellion flared in Abby's eyes. "You're being selfish! Just because you never do anything or go anywhere doesn't mean I have to."

Nora winced. She had lain awake all night mapping out her strategy, and now it was blown to smithereens.

She risked one more touch. She stroked her daughter's cheek before she clasped her hands on top of the table.

"That's not true, honey." She struggled to keep her voice calm. "Under any other circumstances, I'd let you go. Joyce's parents keep a lot of alcohol in the house. At that hour, with boys whose hormones are starting to go haywire, you could get lured into situations too adult for you to handle."

Abby shifted uneasily but lifted her chin. "How would you know?"

"Because I made a mistake once, a bad one. I thought I was grown-up, and tried to act like it."

"Huh? You never make mistakes."

"That's where you're wrong, honey. I make mistakes all the time."

"Oh, right. Like when?"

"Like when I was seventeen. I fell in love with a boy, so deeply that I thought it was okay to have sex with him. It wasn't. I got pregnant with you. Worse, I never told him, not until he came back to town." Nora gazed steadily at her daughter. "He came back to town this week."

Abby paled. "No," she whispered. "No."

She reached out, but her daughter scrambled up, knocking over her chair. "Don't touch me!"

The rejection was expected, but Nora still felt stung. "Abby, listen to me."

"No. Why should I?" Anger flushed her child's face. "My father's Connor?"

"Abby." Nora reached out to her.

"Get away from me." Abby backed away, her movements jerky. "All I am to you is a mistake. That's what you just said." Abby wrapped her arms tightly across her chest. "I'm one huge mistake to you. You don't love me."

Guilt and horror surged through Nora, bringing her to her feet. "No, Abby. How could you think that? I love you with all my heart."

Abby edged toward the porch door. "Not enough to tell me Connor was my father."

She halted her advance. She willed her voice to be calm. "No. But I had my reasons. It turned out I was wrong, but at the time I did what I thought was best."

Abby sneered. "Oh, yes. My mother, The Judge. Everything by her rule book."

"Abby!" Her daughter's bitterness coated her, ate at her like acid. "I don't deserve that."

On a deep shattering sigh, Abby's temper dissipated. She sniffed, a single tear trickling down her cheek. "No, Mom. You deserve a lot worse." She turned and flung open the door.

One hand raised to knock, Connor stood on the stoop. In his other arm he cradled a gigantic pink teddy bear with a swath of purple ribbon tied in a bow around its neck. He took one look at Abby's tearstained face and smiled crookedly. "I guess your mother told you." He thrust out the stuffed toy. "Here, this is for you."

Abby swiped her arm across her eyes. "I'm not a baby!" She pushed past Connor. "I hate both of you! You've ruined my life!" She ran down the steps, across the yard and disappeared into the woods.

Connor slowly lowered the bear and cleared his throat. "Well, that went well."

Nora, her heart breaking, brushed past him, but he grabbed her elbow.

"Hey, where are you going?"

"After my daughter."

"Give her some space. She's had a shock."

"What would you know about children?" She jerked free.

He plopped the bear in a chair. "Damn little, through no fault of my own."

She could still hear Abby screaming all those hateful things. And the man responsible had the audacity to stand there and decry any blame?

"Of all the reprehensible remarks. This is *all* your fault." Raw anguish pumped through her, and like a wounded animal, she lashed out. "I've never fought with Abby. You haven't been back in town for even a week and you've already destroyed everything I love."

"That's not fair." His eyes were like lightning. "You've played your role in this little disaster. My life hasn't been unscathed."

"Good." She moved toward the door, but he blocked her. She shoved him, but he didn't budge.

"Abby will be fine. She went into the woods."

"And that's okay? It'll be dark soon and she's only eleven."

"I'll go after her."

"Over my dead body."

She stabbed him in the chest with her fingernail and took dark pleasure at his wince of pain before his hand covered hers, preventing further attack. She angled her chin in defiance. "Let go of me. You don't know where to look."

"Sure I do. She likes to hang out at our place."

Our place. Where she had found both joy and heart-break.

"No, that's not possible." She had never shown the spot to anyone else, not even her sisters. The last time she had visited it was the day she'd learned she was pregnant. There, hidden from prying eyes, she had given in to her fear and cried.

"How do you know?"

"While on walks with Bran, I've seen her scoot into the clearing." He shrugged. "I've respected her need for privacy like I did yours."

She frowned. "What do you mean?"

"I used to watch you there."

Raw panic skated down her back. What had he seen all those years ago, what secrets did he know? She tried to slip free of his grasp. He only gripped her hand tighter, drawing her closer to him.

"I first spotted you when we were ten. I was walking in the woods and saw you disappearing down the other path. I was curious about the new girl in town, so I followed you. I hid behind the underbrush by the old oak tree."

He slowly rubbed a thumb over her knuckles. "I saw you crying."

Mortification curled into a hot tight ball in Nora's stomach. "You spied on me?"

Connor's smile was faint. "Hey, I was only a kid, remember? I was fascinated, because I couldn't imagine what had upset such a pretty girl. I thought maybe one of the kids had teased you about being new. Whoever had hurt you, I was prepared to beat the daylights out of him. Just when I was ready to rush into the clearing, you sobbed out, 'Mother.'"

Under the gentle rain of his words, Nora's anger began to soften and fade. This time, when she shifted, he released her.

"I had heard all the stories about your mother. You and your sisters had been hot gossip for weeks." He briefly touched her face. "I understood then. I knew what it was like to want your parent's love but not be able to have it. I left you alone. I understood all too well the need for privacy.''

His smile flashed. ''After that, I continued to watch you from time to time. I couldn't figure you out. Instead of playing with some dumb doll with the other girls, you would go there and sit for hours. It got so the first thing I would do before doing my chores on the farm was to check to see if you were here. Then at night, before I headed home, I would look again to make sure you were gone.''

He stepped away and paced the floor. ''I came to view myself as your protector. Watching over you from a distance to make sure no harm came to you.''

His words continued to wrap around her.

''Then before I knew it, you were this beautiful young woman. One day you dropped your books in the school hallway, looked at me with those gray eyes, and I was lost. When you led me to your special spot, I knew what it meant for us to be there. I've never forgotten what we shared, and I've never forgotten you.''

He shoved his hands into his pockets. ''Look, Nora. I can't undo the past twelve years. We both made mistakes. But I think we should put our anger behind us for the sake of Abby.''

Nora took a long steadying breath. ''You're right.''

From his startled glance, she gathered he hadn't expected her ready agreement. He stopped at the refrigerator door and studied the pictures. ''I've never been in the house before. Is this a picture of you and your sisters?'' He pointed to the one taken of them in their new winter coats.

''Yes.'' His comment pricked her conscience. Connor had never been inside because she had never

brought him home. Their meetings had been clandes-
tine, confined to the forest.

Her voice was a whisper. "I'm sorry I never invited
you in."

He shrugged and bent closer to study another photo.
"It doesn't matter."

But it did matter to him, she realized. She took a
tentative step, then another, until she stood alongside
him. Risking a glance at his face, she saw that his jaw
was as chiseled as the stone figures her aunt had
carved. He was looking at the picture of her with Abby,
dressed in her soccer uniform and beaming with pride.

"This kitchen was always the heart of our lives with
Aunt Abigail. It was the place she ushered us into when
we showed up on her porch step." She paused, remembering that bitter scary night.

"Here, she baked pan after pan of cookies to greet
us after school, fixed endless mugs of hot chocolate
and fed us with meals and stories. Her life was totally
upended by our arrival, but she never minded. We were
never alone, not even when she sculpted. We had only
been here a few days when she created *Sisters Three*
just for us. She never sold it, despite the fact she had
offers to buy it and could have used the money. Before
that night, we had never had a sense of belonging anywhere. Abigail fashioned the sculpture of our hands
and molded us into a family."

Her smile was wistful. "I wish she was alive now.
She would know what to do."

Connor put his hands on her shoulders and squeezed.
"Abigail was a good woman, and so are you. You've
done a great job with Abby." He regarded her with
searching gravity. "I admit I don't have a great mother

to follow as an example, but Ed Miller taught me about responsibility.''

His fingers tightened. ''You're not in this alone anymore. I want to be a part of Abby's life. If you give me a chance, I think we can find a way together.''

A chance to be a father. He hadn't said the words, but they were there, hanging between them. She nodded.

He let his hand fall. ''So how do you want to go about handling Abby?''

She cast a worried glance toward the window. It was dusky outside. ''It's getting late. I think one of us should go after her.''

''Let me. It'll give me an opportunity to talk with her. I'll bring her home.''

''All right.'' It was hard to let him go, but she needed to start trusting him with Abby. She cleared her throat. ''About spending time with her….''

Connor averted his face. ''I had planned to take her to that new Disney movie Friday night.'' He hooked his thumbs through his belt loops. ''I guess that's not going to happen now.''

He wanted to take Abby to a children's cartoon. That would score as many points as the teddy bear had. Nora bit her lip, hard, to keep back a chuckle. When she was sure she could speak, she carefully framed her question. ''How do you feel about pizza?''

He looked at her, a faint smile playing across his face. ''I feel great about it if we're talking Sonny's with everything on it.''

''No anchovies.''

The smile spread into a wicked grin. ''I don't know if I can lower my standards.''

She scowled. ''You will if it means going with Abby

and me Friday night before the football game and bonfire."

Connor pushed away from the bench. "It's a date. I'll pick you up at six." He strode across the room to the door, where he hesitated and then turned. "Nora?"

"Yes?"

"Thanks." Without waiting for her reply, he disappeared.

She rubbed the heel of her hand over her heart. The magic was too late for her, but not for her daughter.

I hate them, I hate them, I hate them.

Abby's thoughts synchronized with the pounding of her heart. Heedless of her safety, she raced along the forest path. Twigs, vines and brambles scratched at her legs and arms. Still, she ran.

Hate them, hate them, hate them. Her breathing grew shallow as the frost-nipped air burned her lungs. Sweat beaded on her forehead, and her T-shirt clung to her chest. One more reason not to stop, for if she did, the late-afternoon chill would chase away all heat. And she wasn't ready for that.

She pumped her arms harder.

At the split in the path, Abby veered toward the lake. She had nowhere else to go. Couldn't talk to her aunts. They'd side with Mom. She had no one, no one at all.

The hot aching lump in her chest ripped free with a sob. She burst into the clearing of the Miller gravesite.

Too late, she spotted the boy sitting at the water's edge. This was her place, her special spot. He had no right to be here.

Abby slowed to retreat to the forest's shelter. However, she stubbed her toe on the upraised root of an oak tree and fell to her knees.

"Ow! A sharp pain shot through her left leg. She crumpled to her side and clasped her knee.

Suddenly strong hands were prying hers loose. "Here, let me see." The boy sounded impatient.

Abby muffled a fresh sniffle and swiped her arm across her eyes. She knew that voice almost as well as she knew her own. After all, she'd been dreaming of him since she saw him in the hallway at the start of the school year.

Terrific. Add complete humiliation to her growing list of life's disasters. Crouched beside her was none other than Tony Gennaro, the coolest boy in town.

She blinked and stared into his dark eyes. Oh, man, why did he have to see her like this?

"Are you all right, kid?"

Indignation stiffened her back and spiked her tone. "I'm not a kid, Tony Gennaro. I'll be in junior high next year."

"Right." Tony's smile was dazzling white against his bronzed skin.

"Well, Abby, do you think you can stand?"

He knew her name. She gaped at him.

"Hey!" He snapped his fingers in front of her nose. "Did you hit your head? I asked if you could stand."

"Oh. Sure." Abby rose too quickly and wobbled from the throbbing pain in her knee. Strong hands caught and steadied her. Instead of swooning, she peered at her knee. It didn't look as bad as it felt. Only a little blood oozed from a gash. It should be all right for her soccer game on Saturday.

"Do you need help getting home?"

Her heart did a slow back flip. She brought out the smile she'd spent hours practicing in the mirror. "If you don't mind, Tony. My knee *is* a little sore and stiff.'' She sagged ever so slightly.

"Put your hand around my waist."

Her life could end at this very moment. In a daze Abby complied with his order.

He circled his arm around her shoulders and anchored her to his side. "Let's go." They entered the woods. "Why were you running like a maniac?"

Abby averted her face. "I don't know what you're talking about."

"Come off it. I heard you crashing through the forest long before you entered the clearing. You've got leaves in your hair and brambles all over your clothes. What gives?"

She shrugged. "Nothing."

"Nothing put the tears on your face?"

"None of your business."

"Suit yourself. I just thought…"

"You thought what?"

"Someone may have been picking on you."

"Naw." Abby suddenly needed to talk to someone. "I had a fight with my mom."

"Is that all?"

"Well, thanks a lot!" She withdrew her arm. "I can walk the rest of the way by myself."

"Hey, don't be so prickly." Tony tightened his hold and kept her hobbling beside him. "Me and my folks fight all the time."

Abby couldn't remember ever fighting with her mother before. She couldn't imagine having this roiling sensation in her stomach on a daily basis.

"Doesn't it bother you?"

"Naw. We Gennaros like to yell."

She didn't. This was the first time she had never

shouted at her mother. She didn't know how to face her again.

"After you fight, how do you make up?"

"We laugh and say we're sorry."

"Oh."

They reached the fork in the path. Coming toward them was Connor.

Her father.

She wanted to cry, she wanted to hide, she wanted to run to him.

"Abby." Connor rushed forward and knelt beside her. "What happened?" He glared at Tony. The boy returned the glare.

"I was running and fell. Tony found me and was helping me home. It was my fault. I wasn't looking where I was going." Abby's explanation came through chattering teeth. She was cold, now that she wasn't close to Tony.

The tense lines bracketing her father's mouth eased. "I see." He rose and held out his hand. "Thanks, Tony. I'll take care of Abby from here."

The boy shook his hand and stared at Abby. "Will you be all right with him?"

Connor took off his jacket and wrapped it around her shoulders. Before she could stammer out a thanks, he swept her up in his arms. She gasped and grabbed his shoulders. She felt so small and so very high up.

"Don't worry, son. Abby's safe with me. She's my daughter." Connor cradled her close to his chest and began to walk toward the farmhouse. Abby peeked over his shoulder, saw Tony's startled expression and nodded. Then the rhythm of Connor's stride and the warmth of his jacket started to ease aside her aches and pains, replacing them with weariness. She barely had the energy to hold her head erect.

"Abby, it's all right to lay your head against my shoulder. I won't hold it against you."

Too tired to argue, she rested her cheek on his chest. She felt safe, protected, much the way she often felt in her mother's embrace. Yet different somehow.

A tear trickled down her face as she listened to the steady beat of her father's heart for the first time in her life.

Chapter Six

"Connor, I don't wanna go to the doctor."

"Tough."

It could make a man's head spin to hear how fast his daughter could go from sounding like a woman of the world to a whining five-year-old.

From the moment they'd left that Gennaro kid, Abby had complained nonstop. She'd even fought him about getting into his truck, despite the fact she'd about keeled over with pain when he'd set her on her feet.

Even as he turned onto Maple Street, she was moaning for the umpteenth time about the doctor. The only time she had hushed for even a second had been when he called Nora on his cell phone to let her know where he was taking Abby.

He slowed the truck so as not to miss the clinic's sign. "Doc Sims is taking a look at that knee."

"I have an important soccer game Saturday. We're playing our arch rivals, the Pantherettes."

"All the more reason to get medical attention. You won't be kicking anything if that knee stays the size of a grapefruit."

"I'm fine."

In the dim gloom of the cab, Connor saw Abby cross her arms.

"Quit sulking." He pulled into a spot along the curb. "Wait here until I make sure the doctor's in."

He turned up his collar against the night air, walked to the blue-painted door and raised his hand to ring the after-hours bell. Years ago, Doc Sims, a widower, had moved to the second floor of his clinic. Connor spotted a sign in the window and squinted at the scrawled message: "Elders meeting at Church." He cursed and returned to the truck.

Abby looked ecstatic. "Not there, huh?"

"He's at the church."

"You're taking me home?"

"Nope. To the church."

"But Pastor Devlin's there."

"Yep."

"Does she…"

"If she doesn't know already, she will soon enough. Don't worry. You don't have to hug her and call her Grandma. Unless you want to see the rest of her hair turn white from shock."

He was gratified to earn the first giggle from his daughter since Sunday. He pulled into the curved drive and parked behind a line of cars. He got out, opened the passenger door and held out his arms. After a brief hesitation, Abby scooted to the edge of the seat so he could lift and carry her. She looked up at him, and once more he experienced a slight shock. He couldn't believe he was holding his daughter.

This is my child. My child with Nora.

He marveled at how light she was. What would it have been like to carry her as a baby?

At the entrance he paused, checked his dirt-caked boots and carefully scraped the soles on the mat. He smiled wryly. Some habits never die, especially those ingrained with pain.

With his shoulder, Connor pushed open the ornately carved maple door and stepped into the vestibule. He paused at the Madonna-and-child statue resting under the stark glare of an overhead light. This was a new addition to the church's collection.

"That's Grandmom's statue," Abby said with pride.

"I figured."

"How? Oh, right, the plaque."

Connor smiled. "There's that. But Abigail always sculpted with such smooth flowing lines. You can recognize her pieces because of her trademark spirit."

And doubly so with this work. He always thought the *Sisters Three* was the finest sculpture he'd ever seen, but now he wasn't so sure. Joy radiated from the madonna's face as she looked at the baby she held. Nora would have looked at their daughter in the same way, he knew. Filled with pride and wonder.

Connor inhaled painfully at his sudden insight slashed through him. He was looking at Nora and Abby. Abigail had molded their forms for all eternity to see.

He experienced a bitter rush of resentment. He had missed out on so much; he could only experience his daughter's childhood through the eyes of others.

"That's you and your mom."

Abby squirmed in his arms, half with delight, half with embarrassment. "Yeah."

He tightened his grip on his child, as if by holding her closely he could fill the hollow ache in his chest. Abigail McCall had captured the essence of a mother and child alone, with no husband or father to watch over them. What would Abigail have sculpted if he had never left?

What would you have done if you had known Nora was pregnant? he asked himself for the hundredth time since last night's bombshell. *I'd have taken her with me,* was his gut reaction.

It would have been his only option. To remain would have meant the financial ruination of her family.

But would she have gone with him? Probably not. Even back then, he had realized that Nora's love for him would never equal her love for her sisters and aunt. He wouldn't have had a chance.

Yet, if he'd known he was going to be a father, would he have stayed and risked everything? He studied the statue. Moonlight barely filtered through the triple lancet windows over the door. A cool muted rainbow of color splashed over the sculpture. Behind the pedestal, a shimmering shadow was cast onto the white wall as if a figure were watching over the mother and child.

"Are you going to stand here all night?" Abby sounded peevish.

He couldn't know what he would have done in the past, but he could determine his future course. He moved to the inner doors and shoved them apart.

Several people sitting in the front pews swiveled their heads. Sheila Devlin, standing before the dais, crossed her hands. "I'm in the middle of a meeting,

Connor. Please leave.'' The presence of her parishioners kept her voice to a thin tone of civility.

Abby's hands tightened around his neck. He smiled at her in reassurance. "I have a medical emergency for Doc Sims.'' He strode down the white-carpeted aisle.

Everyone rose. He knew Wilbur Ames and Doc Sims. A familiar-looking man about his age stood near them.

Wilbur rushed forward. "What have you done to her? Abby, did this man hurt you?''

Connor's rage at the accusation was immediate and potent, but he put a chokehold on it. He turned to Doc Sims and ignored everyone else in the room. "Abby fell and cut her knee. Doc, could you take a look at it, please?''

Although age had taken its toll, Doc Sims moved fast when he had to. "Sure, son. Put her on this seat.''

Connor complied and stood clear, but not before he stroked Abby's cheek to reassure her.

"See here, boy.'' Wilbur shoved him. "You leave that girl alone.''

Connor grabbed Wilbur by his shirtfront and jerked the man to his toes. "Back off, Ames.''

Wilbur's jowls quivered, but he managed to bluster, "As principal and church elder, I demand to know what you're doing with that girl at this time of the night.''

Connor felt Nora's presence moments before the others did. Would she tell the truth before this assembly? Or would she try to control the situation and preserve her secret a while longer?

He couldn't afford to give her the chance. If they stood any chance of making it as parents for their daughter, it was time for them all to come out of the dark. He didn't want to be anybody's secret anymore.

He twisted Wilbur's shirt a bit tighter, bringing the man's frightened eyes back to him. "Abby's my daughter, and I have every right to be with her. Don't I, Nora?"

The nave was so quiet that one could hear a penance whispered.

Pale but composed, Nora brushed past him to kneel by Abby. Over her shoulder she looked him right in the eye. She spoke, her voice cool and clear. "Yes, Connor, you have every right as her father."

"Thank you." Connor felt relieved at Nora's acknowledgment. He watched his mother, who had climbed onto the dais to stand behind her lectern. When he saw the fury in her face, he had his answer.

His mother had known the truth all along.

Yet before he had time to absorb all the implications of this, Sheila's patrician features smoothed except for a cruel predatory smile. He was familiar with the expression. The other shoe was about to fall.

The unidentified man, whose expensive navy-blue suit indicated that he meant business, came forward to stand by the pew. "Nora, is it true?"

She glanced up, regret etched on her face. "Yes, David."

Oh, hell, Connor thought. Why hadn't he seen this one coming? He hadn't recognized David Millman, the man Nora was dating.

And he was instantly jealous. Although he knew his reaction was irrational, Connor didn't like to think of any man seeing Nora. She was his.

His former classmate turned and proffered his hand.

"Connor, it's good to see you again. Congratulations, you've got a terrific daughter."

"David, thanks." They shook hands.

David nodded to him and then the group. "If you'll all excuse me, I've got some paperwork at the bank." He strode up the aisle.

Connor studied the rigid set of Nora's shoulders while she spoke with Doc Sims as he examined Abby's knee. Old Ed Miller always said when you cast a stone into the lake you couldn't control the ripples. Judging by the looks and whispers spreading around them, Ed had been right.

The doctor glanced up. "I don't think it's serious, but I want to take an X ray. We need to get her to the clinic."

Connor crossed to the bench and carefully lifted Abby. He carried her down the aisle, ignoring everyone's stares. Nora caught up and walked stiffly beside him.

Outside, they hurried to his truck. "I'll get the door." She climbed in and Connor handed her Abby, who immediately curled into her mother's arms.

He swung into the driver's seat and drove in silence to the clinic. After leaving Abby with Dr. Sims in the examination room, he and Nora sat in the waiting room. He stretched his legs out and shot Nora a dour glance. If her clenched lips and drawn features were any indication, he was in for it.

"Why don't you go ahead and say what you're thinking?"

"Why didn't you call me immediately?" Her voice was low, accusatory.

"I'm sorry. I didn't think of it." He wouldn't admit to the fear he had first felt when he'd found Abby. "My only thought was to get her to the doctor. I did call you from the truck,'' he added in defense.

''Didn't think or didn't want to miss out on the opportunity?''

''What?''

''When you discovered the doctor would be at the elders' meeting at the church, you didn't call me. Are you sure you didn't want to seize the chance to tell the whole town you're Abby's father?''

Shock rocketed through him, followed by anger. He jumped to his feet; Nora followed suit.

''Damn you, Nora. I didn't set you up.''

''No, you just embarrassed me. Did you for one second consider that a man I care about was present for that scene? Did it ever occur to you that there were some people I might want to tell in private?''

Guilt broke through his temper. ''David Millman. You care for him?''

Nora turned away. ''He's been good to me and Abby. We…went out a few times. Nothing serious, but he's been a friend. He deserved better.''

He raised his hand toward her, then let it fall. ''I'm sorry. Things got out of control. When Wilbur accused me of injuring Abby—''

She spun. ''He what?''

''He thought I was responsible.''

''He's an idiot.''

''I agree.''

He felt the tension in the room ease. This time he risked touching her, just a light stroke over her hair. ''I am sorry, Nora.''

She backed away. ''I'm sure you are, Connor, but that doesn't change the fact that announcing you're Abby's father wasn't your decision alone.''

"Nora, Connor." Wiping his hands, Doc Sims stood in the doorway. "Abby's knee is only a sprain. You can take her home now."

After one cool glance at Connor, Nora walked out of the room.

Connor jammed his hands into his pockets. If there was cold comfort to be taken from this rotten night, it was that Nora hadn't believed that he could hurt Abby.

That, and the fact that she hadn't said she loved David Millman.

Nora's knuckles were white from her death grip on the steering wheel by the time she reached the Miller farm. She would enjoy stuffing the farm's land survey someplace other than Connor's hand.

Connor, who had turned her life upside down. Again.

She was exhausted after a sleepless night, and her simmering emotions were once more close to flash point. He hadn't been satisfied with merely destroying her reputation last night; no, he'd had to rub it in today by having her play gofer. Coward. He didn't even have the nerve to call her with his request. Instead, he had called her boss, who had promptly passed the chore to her.

Delivery girl, was she? She was going to deliver a message loud and clear. One she hadn't been able to deliver last night.

The gossip had run through the town like wildfire, and by morning everyone knew. No sooner Nora had entered her office than the staff had pelted her with a barrage of questions. "How's Abby? Oh, thank goodness, no broken bones. Not even stitches? Isn't that amazing. Will she be able to play Saturday?"

That would have been easy to handle, but the questions didn't stop there.

"And what's this about Connor being her father? Aren't you the secretive one? All these years and you never let anyone know. Are you two going to get married now?"

With a cool gaze Nora had asked her secretary to get her a cup of coffee and then fled to the sanctity of her office. After slamming her door, she had pressed shaking fingers to her eyes. She was once more the town's number-one spectacle, just as she had been twelve years ago as an unwed pregnant girl.

Nora gritted her teeth and prayed to the patron saint of auto suspensions as her car bounced over the deep ruts. At the final bend, her mouth fell open. Trucks and other utility vehicles lined the clearing. She pulled to the end and got out. What were all these cars doing here? Her heels promptly sank into the churned dirt.

Great. Chalk up another ruined pair to Connor. Won't he be surprised to see a charge for shoes when he got his bill from the law firm? She stalked around the side of the farmhouse and stopped in amazement. Metal machines, radiating like spokes, shone in the late afternoon sun. To her right, a bulldozer toppled an old rickety shed with a crash. Crews cleared the remnants of outbuildings already razed. The smell of diesel fuel and turned earth permeated the air.

Yellow tape and orange plastic cones cordoned off one lone shed. That must be where Abby's cat and kittens lived, she thought. A huge form heaved itself up from its position in front of the shed door and ambled over to her. Despite her tenuous hold on her temper, Nora couldn't help but smile. "Hello, Bran. Connor got you consigned to guard duty over the kittens?"

The dog uttered a deep-timbered *woof* and bumped her hand with his head. She took the hint and rubbed behind his ears. His tail wagged furiously. "I don't suppose you can track down the weasel who owns you?" The dog's head swung. She followed the line of his nose and spotted Connor by the nursery, talking to two men who wore shirts with pocket protectors and ties. County inspectors, she decided.

"Bran, stay." At her command, the dog turned, walked to the shed and plopped across the door again. A female crew member gave him one look and gave the building a wide berth.

Nora set her shoulders and walked over to Connor. "Mr. Devlin, a word with you."

Connor broke off and swung to face her. "Nora, about time. Do you have the survey? These men are from Franklin County, and they're saying I can't build here. Something about an easement." He turned and gestured to her. "Gentlemen, this is *my* attorney, Ms. McCall. Nora, meet Smith and Wesson."

The shorter man clenched his jaw, "My name's Weissman."

"Whatever. I've got crews waiting, and their time is my money. Nora, the survey."

How had this man ever succeeded in business? She flashed her best client smile. "Mr. Smith, Mr. Weissman." She proffered her hand and both men shook it. "What seems to be the problem?"

Weissman answered, "Nora McCall? You're the one who fought against the annexation and won, aren't you?"

Nora's cheeks warmed. "I merely represented the interests of Arcadia Heights. All credit belongs to the townspeople and their hard work."

Smith and Weissman exchanged looks of disbelief. She recognized Smith, a man in his early thirties with the build of a beanpole, from Saturday's shopping crowd. He'd bought a pink glazed frog for his daughter.

He cleared his throat. "Uh, Ms. McCall. On the old surveys on file at the courthouse, there's an easement for power lines across this property. Mr. Devlin intends to erect one of his greenhouses right on the easement. He can't do that."

"'Old,' gentlemen, is the operative word." She un-zipped her briefcase and hauled out a thick manila folder. She thrust the case at Connor. After he grabbed it, she flipped through the documents. She knew the Miller file inside out. "Here." She pulled loose a sheet of faded parchment and displayed it.

"Forty years ago, when Mr. Miller, the former owner, purchased this farm, he also paid Franklin County the sum of one hundred dollars. In exchange for that, the government released its easement. This transaction is documented and recorded. You've must have missed it on the microfilm. Easy enough to do with the archaic index system over at the courthouse."

With a look of relief, Connor rocked back on his heels. "I told you there was a mistake."

Weissman scanned the page. "This looks legal."

"It's notarized." Nora pointed to the seal and then frowned. She hadn't noticed before that the waiver bore no recording stamp. Hadn't Charlie filed the release? This was serious.

"Yes, well." Weissman looked up. From the gleam in his eye, she knew he had noted the lack of the re-cording, as well. "It does appear we *might* have made a mistake. We'll have to verify this back at the office, of course. May I take the easement with me?"

Nora plucked the document from his fingers. "No, but if you give me a card, I'll be happy to fax you a copy first thing in the morning." She knew these bureaucrats. Entrust an original document to them and it'd be lost in the office paper shuffle forever. She needed to speak with Charlie. Surely he had recorded everything needed to clear title when he had handled Ed's affairs.

Weissman dropped his hand. "Fine. We'll be in contact with you. In the meantime, your client can't build here, not yet."

Frustration dug deep grooves in Connor's face. "We're all set to till and lay the pipes for the main greenhouse."

"Till away," Smith snapped. "But you do so at your own risk. If this waiver isn't valid, you'll have to tear down anything you've built, plus pay a stiff fine." The two inspectors marched away.

"That was interesting," Nora murmured. "Where did you go to business school? The University of How to Make Enemies?"

Connor rounded on her. "This section is the straightest line to lay the utilities needed for the main greenhouse. The other outlying buildings are already under construction." He jerked his thumb at the framework. "It'll cost me a bundle to move this structure off the easement. I showed Charlie the blueprints and he approved the construction plans. You weren't much help just now."

"Don't snap at me, Connor Devlin. I've had a rotten day. I didn't come here to save your hide. I've come to shred it."

His chin jutted. "Spoiling for a fight? Fine. I think I can arrange one." He spun on his heels and yelled,

"Cliff, send everyone home until the inspectors get their heads screwed on straight." He grabbed her elbow. "Come on."

She jerked free. "I don't appreciate the machismo act. Where are you hauling me?"

"The nursery, where we can have some privacy."

"Fine." She stormed past him.

Tony Gennaro burst out of the woods.

"Now what?" Connor muttered.

Tony spotted them and in midstride gathered himself together. He slowed and affected a nonchalant swagger.

"Mr. Devlin, I need to talk with you."

"About what?" Connor held out his hand. The boy hesitated before shaking it.

Nora noticed that the boy looked as if he had been running a great distance. Something was wrong. Her heart clutched. "Aren't you Tony Gennaro?"

"Yes, ma'am."

"Why have you been running? Is there a problem?"

The boy jammed his hands into his front pockets. He flashed a beseeching look at Connor. "I was hoping to talk with Mr. Devlin alone, but since you're both Abby's parents…"

Connor stilled. "What's wrong, son?"

Tony flushed. "I really shouldn't say anything. None of my business, but I thought you'd want to know that the kids were pretty rough on Abby today at school. Name-calling and that kind of stuff. About you, Mr. Devlin…" The boy cleared his throat. "Anyway, none of the teachers stopped it, including Mr. Ames."

"Where's Abby now?" Connor demanded.

"She's at the shop." Tony shrugged when they both stared at him. "I walked her there after school was out."

"Tony, thanks. For everything." Connor squeezed his shoulder and the boy left.

Nora's anger was now blade-sharp. "Connor, this is all your fault." She knew exactly what kind of "stuff" Tony had meant. She and her sisters were expert receivers of the mean, unthinking insults of schoolmates. Later she'd get the teachers' names and have a word with each one. They were supposed to protect the children. As for Ames, she'd haul him before the school board.

She stormed toward the farmhouse. While it would be quicker to go through the woods, her car was here, which meant a return trip. And she wasn't in the mood to deal with Connor again.

"My fault?" He caught up with her. "Right, Nora. Heap the blame on me if it makes you feel better." With his long sure stride, Connor reached the drive before her and stood next to her car.

"What do you think you're doing?"

"Like it or not, Abby needs both of us right now."

"No. What *my* daughter needs is for you to leave her alone."

"That's what *you* want. Big difference, Nora."

"Whatever. Get your own ride. You're not going with me." She opened her door, slid inside and slapped her palm on the door locks. She turned the key in the ignition, gunned the engine and spun the car around, spraying mud. When she checked her rearview mirror, she saw Connor standing.

Not a spot on him.

Nora's rotten luck continued to hold. She rushed through the front door of Kilning You Softly and landed in the thick of things. At the tables painting pottery were the members of the Arcadia Heights Monday Night Bridge Club.

The bridge club got together faithfully every week—not to play cards, but to tear apart anyone in the town who had caught their notice. Truth, honor and principles need not apply.

Tonight's self-appointed virtuous and vulturous members were Wilbur Ames and his wife, Nancy, Geraldine Millman, David's mother, and the group's latest fledgling, Molly Deutscher, wife of the town's librarian.

From the audible gasps and ill-disguised stares, she could almost hear their thoughts.

Town's "Bad Girl" at twelve o'clock.

Let them gawk. There would be no repeat performance of the Connor-Nora drama tonight. She scanned the room. Eve, standing behind the counter, nodded toward the back. Abby was in the kiln alcove. She would get her and go up to the house for a cozy mother-daughter talk.

Her plan was short-lived. The door slammed open and Connor strode in.

Over at the cash register Eve muttered, "Oh, great. Here comes the preacher's son."

Connor halted before Nora, so close she could have sworn an electrical current arced between them. "Where is she?"

The mother in Nora waffled over letting this man near her wounded daughter. The lawyer in her honed in on the conversation behind her.

"Come back to stir up more trouble, Devlin? Didn't you do enough of that at the church?" Disdain failed to conceal the excitement in Wilbur's voice.

"He's not happy unless he's breaking his mother's

heart. Can you imagine how humiliated she is now that everyone knows about..." Nancy Ames gave Nora a significant look.

Only the muscle flexing along Connor's jaw disturbed the granite of his face. He walked over to the table.

"I don't give a damn if you call me names, but you'll answer to me if you hurt either my daughter or Nora."

He turned, walked over to Nora and slid his arm around her waist. She could feel the tension running through his body.

The realization hit her hard. He did know what it meant to be the subject of others' slurs. He had shared the same pain.

How often had she watched him hide behind an impenetrable devil-may-care facade? As a youth, he had faced the world with a sneering smile, jutting chin and a flippant quip. Maybe together they would be able to counsel Abby and show her a better way to face the world.

Her heart pounding, Nora whispered, "She's in back."

Connor wanted to heave a sigh of relief. He hadn't been sure of how Abby would react to the innuendoes. Twelve years spent building his landscaping franchise had given him a tough hide. The whispered snide remarks were like ice pellets—a momentary sting of chill, but not enough to distract him.

With deep satisfaction Connor realized that he and Nora had stood on the edge of a precipice in their new relationship. She had just extended a peace offering.

Warm flesh brushed his fist. Funny, he hadn't realized that he had clenched his hands. Nora's gentle but determined fingers urged his to relax and to intertwine with hers. A sense of well-being and completeness flooded through him when he looked down at Nora's hand linked with his.

"Come on, let's go see Abby."

In the small back room they found the girl wrapping a lizard figurine.

"Abby, are you okay?" Nora asked.

Abby put the figurine down on the worktable, then picked it up again. "I'm fine." She grabbed a pair of scissors and hacked away a swath of the plastic. "What are you doing here?"

Connor leaned against the workbench. "We heard you had a rough day, honey. We were concerned."

"Sure you were."

"Abigail McCall, mind your manners."

Abby's blue eyes clouded with angry tears. "McCall isn't my last name anymore."

Abby Devlin. His name. The prospect made him yearn.

Nora's chin shot up. "It's the name on your birth certificate."

"For how long?"

Connor heard the panic in her voice and shelved his dream for the time being. "Forever, if that's what you want." He clasped her shoulder. "I just want to get to know you, Abby. There's no timetable here, no deadlines to be met in our relationship. Do I hope someday you'll want to use my name? I won't lie to you. Of course I would." He would never pressure her. She had to take his name of her own free will.

A tear slipped down Abby's face. Connor chanced wiping it away with his thumb. "I don't know much about being a dad. Never had one myself. But I know about being a friend, and I sure would like to be yours.''

Her lower lip trembled.

"How about it? Give me a shot?" He waggled his eyebrows. "I'll throw in a ride on my motorcycle."

His reward was Abby's giggle, filling his heart with hope.

Nora interjected, ''Oh, no you won't, Connor Devlin.''

"Mom!"

"That's because she wants the first ride." He winked.

Coming to stand behind Abby, Nora gave her a fierce hug. "We'll discuss the motorcycle later." She nudged the girl. "It's late. Why don't you go up to the house and do your homework? I'll finish up here and join you."

Abby nodded. He saw the nervousness in her eyes and wished he could vanquish it as easily as he had her tears. ''Will I still see you tomorrow?''

He lightly chucked her under the chin. "You bet. I'll pick you up at six."

She flashed a quick grin and darted out the back door, letting in a gust of night air.

Now that they were alone, Connor seemed to be more, well, overwhelming, Nora decided. He leaned against the bench and folded his arms, his gaze intense.

Suddenly nervous, Nora picked up the brightly colored lizard. She remembered Christina assuring the boy who had painted it that the dull colors he dabbled on would transform into vivid hues after glazing. ''Just like a chameleon does.''

Just like the man beside her, Nora thought. She had been expecting Connor to resort to his ways of youthful

defiance with the townspeople. Were his comments to
Abby reflections of the man Connor had become, or
was the youthful Connor still hidden beneath a veneer
of control? And would she be able to find out in time
to avoid pain for Abby?

She was no good with men outside her professional
life. Her experience with Connor had taught her that
much.

She reached for a sheet of brown wrapping paper.
Her hand collided with his. She looked up, and her
breath caught. The glow of the table lamp lit Connor's
bronzed skin with tantalizing warmth. She yearned to
reach out and stroke his flesh.

Blue fire burned in his eyes. If she looked too
deeply, those flames would singe her.

She heard a sigh. Was it his or hers? She didn't care
anymore whether he had changed. Whether he was the
boy she had known or the man she had dreamed of.

His head lowered, his mouth a kiss away. If she
moved her head a fraction, she could drink from it. She
laid her hand against the solid wall of his chest, not
sure if she meant to repel him or brace herself.

She felt a jab of pain. She became dimly aware that
her back was pressed against the counter's edge. Connor grabbed her around the waist and lifted her onto
the bench. In that dazzling moment she could have
sworn she was flying. A soft gasp—half alarm, half
delight—escaped from her. His touch scorched her
through her jeans as he opened her thighs and stepped
between them.

"Nora." His rough voice was a reverent whisper in
the heated hush of the room. "I've missed you."

He nuzzled her neck, his lips doing a soft smooth
glide along her skin. He nibbled at the corner of her

mouth before he sipped at her lower lip as if it were nectar.

Liquefying.

He slid his hands from her waist to her ribcage, to rest below her breasts. Before she realized what she was doing, she raised her arms and linked her fingers behind his neck.

He stepped closer, opening her even more. The kiln hummed with approval. Nora felt as if she was in the presence of a master sculptor, his touch molding a magical response from her body. She craved his next move.

"Nora?" Eve's raised, impatient voice from the shop shattered Nora's sensual haze. "Would you please bring out David Greenfield's lizard? His mom is waiting for it."

The cold shower of reality doused Nora. Her arms stiffened, her hands pushed. Connor stepped back. Hunger still smoldered in his gaze. "We'll finish this later," he promised.

Nora's hand trembled as she picked up the bundle. She couldn't trust herself with this man; she couldn't trust herself to be alone with him. Her body, having felt his touch, his kiss, yearned for more.

No. She was no longer a girl yielding to physical need. She had a child to consider. She couldn't afford to be wrong a second time.

Chapter Seven

Her cowardly boss had left her holding the bag.

Still on a low simmer since her abbreviated conversation with Charlie, Nora stood by the only window in her second-floor office. She stared at the sparse early-Friday-morning traffic on Maple Street. The thick file sat on her desk.

As of seven-thirty, Charlie had been on an impromptu three-day-weekend trip. He'd left her terse instructions—clean up his mess and advise his client. Right. Little did her boss realize she'd been with the same client ten hours and twelve minutes earlier.

Murphy's Law once again prevailed. Break her code of never socializing with the firm's customers outside of business, and look where it had landed her. Stuck in a musty office playing the cool professional with the one man who could make her discard all rational behavior.

How she was to accomplish such a miracle of control, she didn't know. Not when she could still taste him on her lips.

"At this early hour, a man and his woman should be wrapped in each other's arms, holding the day at bay for one more kiss."

He could also read minds. She spun to face him.

"I knocked but no one answered, so I let myself in." Connor strode across the floor. From the determined glint in his eye to the cocky smile curving that incredibly tempting mouth, it appeared that he intended to take up where he had left off last night.

He halted, so close she could smell him, all leather and earth and man. He slipped a deep-red mum into the lapel of her Donegal-tweed jacket. Something inside her bloomed, as fragile and vital as the hothouse flower over her breast.

He hadn't shaved. What would it feel like, his roughened skin against hers? All she had to do was lift her face to find out.

No, you have a job to do. The battle of lawyer versus woman was brief but brutal. The pragmatic attorney won, quashing feminine yearning. The last thing Connor would do after he heard the news was kiss her.

She stepped back and forced a brisk smile. "Good morning, Connor. Thanks for coming over so quickly."

Irritation and concern crossed his features. He grasped her upper arms and stayed any further retreat. "What's wrong, Nora? Is it Abby? You're paler than a lily."

Nora felt herself smile. "I just love it when you talk plant to me. No, Abby's fine."

His hands flexed, relaxed, then released her. She

added a foot of separation between them for good measure.

"Good." He hooked his thumbs through his belt loops. "Why the summons, then?" He winked. "Couldn't wait until tonight to see me?"

Desperate to stave off the inevitable, Nora stalled. "I need coffee. Would you like some?"

"Okay. But I have to make this quick. I left the crew, and if I don't watch them they're apt to lay the foundation for the gift shop where the toolshed should be."

Nora moved to the coffee machine on her credenza.

"I hope you don't mind coffee made from packs. The staff won't be here for another hour, and I haven't mastered the art of measuring loose grains. In fact, my secretary spent an hour showing me how to fill the container with water." Nora gave a start when she looked up and saw him beside her.

His dimple deepened. "It's fine, Nora."

She poured one mug, offered it to him and then filled hers. "Charlie showed up one day holding this fancy machine. He bragged, 'Only the best for my staff.' Later, one of the secretaries learned it was a gift from a grateful client."

Connor took a hefty swallow. "Nora, what's wrong?"

She sniffed the coffee, decided against it and set down her mug. She had delayed long enough. "I have something to show you."

One had to give the man points for courage. He gamely held on to his cup and even braved another sip.

The statuette on the left-hand corner of her desk drew her gaze. *Lady Justice,* as sculpted by Abigail for Nora's law-school graduation present, wielded a sword rather than scales. Had her aunt really seen her with such courage?

Tell him, Nora. She took her courtroom steadying breath.

"The easement release wasn't recorded."

Connor's blank look didn't last long. Comprehension flashed on his face before anger replaced it.

"Explain."

She tugged loose a folder from the file. "Simple. Charlie didn't realize he needed to record the waiver to clear the title. He believed the signed document would suffice."

With a slow controlled movement, Connor set his mug on a legal pad atop the desk. Nora was certain he had wanted to slam the cup down and sent a prayer of thanks to the guardian of antique cherry furniture. Christina had spent hours refinishing it.

"How much trouble am I in?" His intense gaze could have nailed a snake at twenty paces.

She ordered herself not to squirm and assumed her best reassuring expression. "The county recording department won't be open until nine. I'll be at the doors when they do and see to its recording."

"Isn't that like locking the henhouse after the rooster's already had his way?"

"Not for future transactions."

"What if the county denies the release ever occurred?"

She shook her head. "Shouldn't be a problem for two reasons." Nora fanned the thick stack of paper. "Number one. We're fortunate that Charlie's a pack rat. He keeps everything. I've got all the letters from the negotiations."

"And the second reason?"

She allowed herself a small smile of victory. After all, this winning card was one she had discovered during her frantic review of the file after speaking to Charlie.

"I'm glad to see you're so confident about fixing this screwup."

She smirked and laid down her trump card. "You know the county officer who signed the release?"

"What about him?"

"He still holds the same office and—" she paused a second "—he's a longtime friend of my boss. Charlie's going to call him." She had insisted he do that much before he left town. "As soon as I finish recording the original waiver, I'll stop by his office."

Connor rocked on his heels. "How long before I can build?"

"Hopefully within the next week or so." She expected thanks. Instead, she got a contemptuous glare.

He raked fingers through his already tousled hair. "Damn it, Nora, that's not good enough. The project's schedule is tighter than a Gideon's knot."

She folded her arms. "I don't understand. There're always delays in construction, and since this is a landscaping—"

"It's not only that, Nora." Frustration deeply etched his face. "It's also a botanical garden." He jerked a thumb at the window. "In case you haven't noticed, we're well into autumn, with winter frost nipping at our heels. The ground is already the consistency of brick. Every passing day makes tilling harder. Every day of delay means more cost overruns."

"Still, it's not as if there's a magic day when it has to be finished."

"That's where you're wrong. I gave my word and

due to *your* firm's mistake, I may not make good on it.'' He grabbed her. ''But you already know that, don't you? You've seen the will.''

She had never before witnessed Connor so furious. With panic beating wildly in her chest, she stood dead still in his grasp. ''No. Only Charlie has seen it.''

Connor released his hold and ran his hands up and down her arms.

''Sorry.'' He moved to the window. His gaze was pensive. ''Remember Ed's wife?''

Vividly. The first time she had been invited into Lois Miller's kitchen, the middle-aged woman had graciously offered her a plate of fresh-baked sugar cookies. Nora could still remember how the warm cookies had melted in her mouth. Several months later Lois had died from breast cancer.

''Yes.''

''Lois loved roses.''

''I know. Old Ed tended her gardens for years, right up until he died.''

''Their wedding anniversary was May first.''

''How did you know that?''

''The will.''

''Why would their anniversary date be in the will unless...'' She stared at him. ''Ed asked you to build the botanical gardens in tribute to his wife.''

''He wanted the display to be ready by spring. Lois loved seeing daffodils and tulips bobbing in the wind. On his deathbed, Ed called and asked me to carry out his tribute to his wife. I promised him.'' Connor clenched his hands. ''It may not be binding as a legal document, but my word to that man is sacred as any oath to me.''

''Can't you plant in the spring?''

"No, the bulbs have to be planted by first frost."

He faced her, determination glinting in his eyes. "I can only manage a bare-bones operation in that amount of time. But even if I have to strip my other nurseries bare, I will have those gardens he wanted by next spring.

"You're always talking about trust." Connor walked past her to the door. "Ed and I trusted this law firm. I hope you're right when you say you can fix this."

The door slammed.

Nora released her breath. "Thank you for using the law offices of Charles Barnett." She grabbed her purse and rummaged for her car keys. "Quality legal service is our motto." She tossed the Miller file into her briefcase and headed down the hallway. "We aim to please even if it means spending a gorgeous weekend in the dusty bowels of government bureaucracy."

She paused and pressed her forehead against the chilled windowpane of the outer office door. What a mess. However was she going to make it right?

By taking it one step at a time, which meant going to Columbus. Nora twisted the knob and yanked open the door.

With a Swiss Army knife clenched in his teeth, Connor double-checked his watch. Five-twenty. Enough time to unpack this last shipment before heading over to the pottery shop to pick up Nora and Abby for his first date with his daughter. Along the way, he might figure out how to apologize to Nora for his bad temper this morning.

If she was still speaking to him.

Connor removed the knife from his mouth before he could do serious harm to himself. If he thought that he

GIFTS from the Heart

Play and you can get **2 FREE BOOKS** and a **SURPRISE GIFT!**

Play Gifts from the Heart and get 2 FREE Books and a FREE Gift!

HOW TO PLAY:

1. With a coin, carefully scratch off the gold area at the right. Then check the claim chart to see what we have for you — **2 FREE BOOKS** and a **FREE GIFT** — **ALL YOURS FREE!**

2. Send back the card and you'll receive two brand-new Silhouette Special Edition® novels. These books have a cover price of $4.50 each in the U.S. and $5.25 each in Canada, but they are yours to keep absolutely free.

3. There's no catch. You're under no obligation to buy anything. We charge nothing —**ZERO** — for your first shipment. And you don't have to make any minimum number of purchases — not even one!

4. The fact is, thousands of readers enjoy receiving books by mail from the Silhouette Reader Service™. They enjoy the convenience of home delivery... they like getting the best new novels at discount prices, **BEFORE** they're available in stores...and they love their *Heart to Heart* subscriber newsletter featuring author news, horoscopes, recipes, book reviews and much more!

5. We hope that after receiving your free books you'll want to remain a subscriber. But the choice is yours — to continue or cancel, any time at all! So why not take us up on our invitation, with no risk of any kind. You'll be glad you did!

A surprise gift

FREE!

We can't tell you what it is... but we're sure you'll like it! A

FREE GIFT!

Visit us online at
www.eHarlequin.com

just for playing **GIFTS FROM THE HEART!**

DETACH AND MAIL CARD TODAY!

PLAY GIFTS from the Heart

Scratch off the gold area with a coin.
Then check below to see the gifts you get!

YES! I have scratched off the gold area. Please send me the 2 Free books and gift for which I qualify. I understand I am under no obligation to purchase any books as explained on the back and on the opposite page.

335 SDL DNSK   235 SDL DNSF

FIRST NAME

LAST NAME

ADDRESS

APT.#

CITY

STATE/PROV.

ZIP/POSTAL CODE

♥ ♥ ♥ ♥ 2 free books plus a surprise gift

♥ ♥ ♥ 2 free books   ♥ ♥ 1 free book

(S-SE-05/02)

Offer limited to one per household and not valid to current
Silhouette Special Edition® subscribers. All orders subject to approval.

The Silhouette Reader Service™ — Here's how it works:

Accepting your 2 free books and gift places you under no obligation to buy anything. You may keep the books and gift and return the shipping statement marked "cancel." If you do not cancel, about a month later we'll send you 6 additional books and bill you just $3.80 each in the U.S., or $4.21 each in Canada, plus 25¢ shipping & handling per book and applicable taxes if any.* That's the complete price and — compared to cover prices of $4.50 each in the U.S. and $5.25 each in Canada — it's quite a bargain! You may cancel at any time, but if you choose to continue, every month we'll send you 6 more books, which you may either purchase at the discount price or return to us and cancel your subscription.

*Terms and prices subject to change without notice. Sales tax applicable in N.Y. Canadian residents will be charged applicable provincial taxes and GST.

could mend this latest rift with a few smooth lines, then he had a few acres of Everglades swampland to sell himself.

In the faint hope of establishing a momentary truce for Abby's sake, he'd spent the better part of an hour cleaning and polishing his truck and then another thirty minutes slicking himself up. He had planned to stay inside afterward, but the nursery, with its new arrivals, had beckoned him. If he was careful, only his hands would need washing.

Right.

With a ferocious smile, he sliced the blade through a package. The carton fell away, revealing a potted rose. "Hello, sweetheart," he crooned softly. With a critical eye, Connor examined the pruned bush for any breakage. He then checked the greenness of the slender canes and tested the dryness of the potting material.

He moved on to the next mummified bundle on the workbench. Ten minutes later he had five slender rose-bushes freshly watered, fertilized and set up in their new home. Hooking his heel on the leg of a stool, Connor pulled it up to the bench and sat down. He folded his arms and looked around him.

Chaos might reign outside the botanical gardens, but here in his conservatory—the soul of his operation—everything was working. He inhaled deeply of the incense of plants—the fecund smell of soil and moss intermingled with the pungent scent of fertilizer and pesticide.

Connor sighed with contentment and gave himself up to his sanctuary.

The newly activated heating pipes murmured their prayers in the hush of the night. Already, droplets of steam had formed on the wind-chilled glass, baptizing the walls. The aluminum supports arched overhead, dark skeletal fingers holding up the crystal dome. Along its crown a rosary of reflector lamps reverentially illuminated the greenhouse. All around him, the frosty veil of the glazed glass transformed the black night to a platinous brilliance—the color of Nora's eyes in the moonlight.

Connor's gaze rested on the roses in front of him.

Twelve long years, and his dream was finally coming to fruition. Ever since he had landed a job at that nursery in Loxahatchee, Florida, he had been drawn to the painstaking process of creating new roses through cultivation and crossbreeding. When he had completed his daily tasks, he had worked late into the night to learn how to cross-pollinate. It had been years of trial and error to create his masterpiece.

Now he was finally home, the only home he had ever wanted, for the final leg of his long journey: having his own cultivar recognized and listed.

A gray hybrid tea with a white reverse. Stormy purple in the shade, gentle dove-gray in the sunlight, "Nora's Pride" would be as hardy and eloquent as its namesake's defiant eyes, which had haunted him since that day he'd walked away.

His gaze fell to his watch. Five-forty. Time to clean up and collect Nora and Abby. Rising, he paused to run a forefinger along a tender leaf. Come spring he would introduce his Pride to the Rose Hybridizers Association. Not for the first time a mental picture arose of Nora standing by his side to share with him his moment of glory.

A sharp thorn pricked his finger. He swore and jerked his hand away from the cane. A tiny dot of blood welled from the puncture site. What was he doing? Mooning over a future with Nora?

Yes, he was. He might as well resign himself to the idea. One way or the other, she was a part of his life because of the child they shared. He sucked the wound.

How am I going to handle this?

Physical desire was one thing; a future together was another. A mile of misunderstanding separated the two.

And then there was their daughter.

Muttering a curse, he washed his hands, grabbed his jacket and went out into the night.

Sonny's Pizzeria had stood on the corner across from the high school as long as anyone in town could remember. Still owned and operated by the Donatelli family, its decor never changed: red-and-white-checked plastic tablecloths, centerpieces of wine bottles encased in candle drippings and cheaply framed posters of Venice, Florence, Naples and Rome on the walls. To step into the restaurant was to enter a world of warmth, from the spicy aroma of pepperoni and sausage to the good-natured yelling between the staff and the owners.

At her insistence, Abby had taken one side of the booth while her parents shared the other. Nora had never realized how cramped the seats were, not until she sat next to Connor. No matter how compressed she made herself, his thigh pressed against hers, his arm rubbed hers from shoulder to elbow. For some reason, the restaurant was hotter than she remembered.

From Abby's squirming, Nora knew that she also felt ill at ease at this first official family outing. If her daughter slouched any lower in the booth, she would slide underneath the table.

Nora was about to suggest she sit up when the door

opened and Abby bolted upright of her own accord. Nora followed her gaze and saw Tony Gennaro.

Uh-oh. Her mother's antenna went on full alert. She was going to have to watch this one. Abby's infatuation was a clear and future danger.

Tony cut across the room to their table and greeted them. He casually asked Abby, "Do you have time to play a few video games before your pizza is brought out?"

"Mom?"

Nora looked at her watch and nodded. "About ten minutes. Keep an eye out for the pizza."

Abby scooted out.

Connor reached into his pocket and dragged out some change. "Abby, here's some quarters."

Abby turned the full blast of her smile on him. "Thanks, Connor. Come on, Tony."

Nora watched them go into the back room, where Sonny had installed video games.

"Some things never change."

"Like what?" She faced Connor.

He winked. "A boy, a girl and a game machine. Remember?"

Of course she did, but she was amazed that he did. They had come here on their last night together for pizza and games in the back room. He had stood behind her, pressed close, while he guided her hands on the pinball machine.

"The games are more advanced than the ones we used to play." She took a sip of her soda to quench the sudden dryness in her mouth.

"Not all the games, Nora. Some will always be played the same way."

She choked on her drink and clasped a napkin to her

lips. Through watery eyes, she noticed the stares of a few other customers. She turned her head slightly to cut them from her line of sight.

He frowned. "Do they bother you?"

"No." She smiled slightly. "It can never be as bad as the first night that Abigail brought us here. It was your typical Friday-night bedlam, and yet absolute silence fell when we came through the door."

Her skin prickled at the memory of being the center of attention. Eve and Christina had huddled behind Abigail's back, but Nora, her knees shaking, had stood her ground in front. Let them stare.

Connor's gaze was sympathetic. "That must have been rough on you young girls."

"Yes—" Nora folded her used napkin and pulled out a fresh one "—but then Sonny came to the rescue." She laughed softly. "I'll never forget the sight of this enormous man, dressed in a stained apron, barreling from the kitchen and wiping his hands." She mimicked a heavy Italian accent, "'Abigail, *cara mia.* So you bring your gorgeous chicks to me!' He swooped down on me and just about knocked me off my feet with a hug."

"He must have scared you."

"Yes, at first." She had been so startled at being grabbed by a stranger that she'd had to bite her lip to clamp a scream. But Sonny's warmth had seeped past her guard. Even with her youthful cynicism, she had recognized that his gesture was genuine.

"When I smiled, he clasped his hand to his chest and gasped, 'Oh, my heart. Abigail, she's going to be a heartbreaker with that smile.' Then without releasing me, he crouched and peered around Abigail's legs at

Christina and me. 'As will be these precious *bambini.*'"

"When he held out his other arm, Eve threw herself into his grasp while Christina sort of glided into the circle. He then rose with all three of us and called out, 'Hey, everyone, meet Abigail's new family.'" Thirty minutes later a gigantic gooey confection had been placed before the delighted girls. To this day, it was the best pizza Nora had ever tasted. Tangy tomato sauce, a thick fluffy crust and a triple order of cheese. A young girl's version of ambrosia.

"Good memory?"

"Yes, it is."

Connor swept up her pile of used napkins. "Would you excuse me a second?"

"Sure." She slid over to let him out. After he disappeared into the crowd, she scanned the room.

Arcadia Heights's pre-football-game ritual was pizza at Sonny's, and the place was packed tighter than a jar of capers. In the far corner Pastor Devlin held court with the Ameses and David Millman's father and mother. They had been staring at Connor and Nora since their arrival. One table over sat the county inspector Leon Smith and his family; he kept glancing her way as well.

She checked her watch. She wished Connor would return. He hadn't yet asked her about the property, but then, there hadn't been an opportunity to speak in private. By the time he had arrived at the pottery shop to thrust a bouquet of winter-white rosebuds at her, they had been in the throes of closing for the night and she had pressed him into cleaning tables.

Suddenly he was back. "Move over."

She scooted as close to the wall as she could, but

his body still pressed against hers as he sat down. He draped his arm across the back of the bench. Nora leaned forward.

"Connor, before Abby returns—"

"Do you have any good memories of us?"

Flustered, she toyed with her straw. "Of course."

"Such as?" Connor's hand drifted to her nape. In the restaurant there was that moment's lull in the volume level when the jukebox switched from one record to another. An old familiar song began to play, REO Speedwagon's "Can't Fight This Feeling."

"What about this song? Do you remember it?"

She had played it so often that she had worn the tape out. Connor had selected it on the jukebox every time they had come here.

"Of course."

"I had to buy a new tape. Mine fell apart." His fingers toyed with stray wisps of hair, electrifying her skin. "Nora, I've never told you—"

The noise level crescendoed as the kitchen door swung open. Sonny Donatelli rushed out with a steaming pan held high. After pausing by one table to scold an elderly couple to clean their plates, he arrived at their booth. With a flourish he placed the pan on the table.

"Connor, you forget about that wimpy tropical pizza made with pineapple and sink your teeth into my finest."

Abby slid into her seat; her hand collided with Nora's as they both went for the same gooey slice. With a smile Nora let her daughter win. Her hand paused over an empty space. She glared at Connor, who gave her an innocent smile before taking a healthy bite out of what should have been her slice. Nora grabbed for the third piece before any more could disappear.

With a satisfied grunt, Sonny folded his arms. "Connor. I hear you're a fancy gardener now."

Connor wiped his hands. "That's right."

Nora noticed that the couple at the table next to their booth quit talking. She waited until their gazes met hers, then smiled with a show of teeth. The customers blushed and returned to their meal, but Nora knew they were still listening. She turned her attention back to Sonny.

"I hear you're going to be hiring some help," Sonny said.

Connor's shrug plastered his shoulder against hers. Nora wished she had worn a shirt rather than a turtleneck so she could loosen a few buttons.

"That's right." Connor shot an amused glance at his attentive audience. Conversation had died, leaving only the clang of the pizza pans from the kitchen. His voice was clearly audible. "I'll need nine or ten workers for the winter crews. Maybe ten more for the summer, plus staff for the shops."

A murmur rippled through the restaurant. Sonny puffed out his chest. "My sister's oldest boy is looking for an after-school job. He's a good kid. Not afraid of hard work."

"Have him see me Monday afternoon," Connor said.

Sonny grinned. "I'll do that." He wheeled around and scurried back to the kitchen.

Leaning forward to grab another napkin, Nora spotted Leon Smith threading his way toward them. She didn't have to lean far to murmur in Connor's ear, "On advice of counsel, you be civil."

"Mr. Devlin."

Connor nodded. "Smith."

"I was going to call you tomorrow, but I couldn't help overhearing your conversation with Sonny about the number of people you intend to hire."

"You and everyone else in this joint."

Nora couldn't kick, but she could grab the taut flesh on Connor's muscular thigh and pinch. Before she could retreat, his hand captured hers and squeezed. Hard.

The county inspector cleared his throat. "Yes. Well. I have good news for you. Although the easement release wasn't recorded—" his pale-blue gaze flickered to Nora and then back "—the county did enter into an agreement with the former owner and will honor it. You'll be able to resume building at the start of the week."

Connor's fingers flexed over Nora's beneath the table. He extended his hand. "Thank you."

"Sorry for any misunderstanding the other day." Smith gestured. "Excuse me, my family's waiting. Enjoy your evening."

"Nora, what did happen with the easement today?"

Nora ignored Connor's demand while she watched Pastor Devlin summon the inspector.

Great. Sheila Devlin could sniff out a transgression at a hundred paces, and she could certainly worm a confession out of an angel. Any hope of keeping Charlie's blunder confidential faded as the woman fixed her regal smile on the poor unsuspecting inspector. He'd be spilling his guts before Sonny could yell the next "Pizza up."

As the inquisition progressed, Nora watched Wilbur Ames, his face pale, turn and stare with disbelief at

Connor. Satisfaction at Wilbur's slack-jawed expression unfurled within Nora. Wilbur's gaze slid from Connor to Nora. His lips pressed tightly together in disapproval.

Nora forced a sweet smile and leaned back until Connor's body shielded her. What a shortsighted narrow-minded prig Wilbur was. He had continually judged and condemned Connor without ever giving him a chance.

Abby shifted in her seat, dreamily toying with her straw. Who knew what thoughts danced in her daughter's head? But whatever they were, Nora wanted to tend them with loving care.

Once more she studied Wilbur, who was now animatedly talking and gesturing. It didn't take ESP to know what the topic of conversation was. Although she'd set up a meeting at the school next week to address the taunting Abby had been subject to, would that be enough? What would Wilbur and his rigid viewpoints do to her high-spirited creative daughter?

The other members of the school board were regressive, as well; Pastor Devlin's tight control of community affairs ensured a school board that followed her every decree. What the school district really needed was some new blood.

"Hey, earth to Mom. Are you there?" Abby's irritated voice broke into her thoughts. Nora started and realized both Connor and her daughter were frowning at her.

"I asked," Abby said in exaggerated measure, "whether you were ready to leave. It's almost game time and we want to get good seats."

Nora nodded. "Sure. I was just thinking."

Connor grunted as he finished the last slice of pizza.

He wiped his hands. "Now there's something new and exciting."

Nora glared at him. "If you'd give me a chance to finish…"

"I've been trying to get you to *start* for the past few minutes." He winked at Abby.

"I thought I might run for the school board."

Over Abby's groan of dismay, Nora heard Connor whisper into her ear, "That's my girl." His approval sent a pulse of pleasure shooting down her spine.

But then he frowned. "Nora, isn't it only a few weeks until the election? Sheila always kept the date circled in red on her calendar so she could invite candidates over to grill them. Wouldn't the filing period be closed?"

"Oh." Her disappointment was a hard lump in her throat, made even larger when she heard Abby's sigh of relief. Was her daughter embarrassed by her?

"Abby, honey. Why wouldn't you want me to run?"

"Just because."

"Because what?"

"The other kids would get on my case."

"Why would they do that?"

"Mom, it's so obvious." Abby rolled her eyes. "The school board hires the teachers, right?"

"Yes."

"How do you think the teachers treat the kids of school-board members?"

"Like all the others?"

"Wrong, Mom. Nothing's too good for them. They're real teachers' pets."

Nora sighed. "Well, buck up. Tragedy averted. It's too late for me to file."

"Not for write-in's."

"What?" She faced Connor.

His eyes twinkled. "I just remembered about write-in candidates. There wouldn't be any filing required for them."

"And little to no chance of winning."

He shrugged. "Take a candidate who saved the town a ton of taxes by preventing the annexation. Throw in a few signs and a little grassroots campaigning, and who knows? You might find yourself the victor come the first Tuesday in November."

She swallowed. "Do you really think so?"

His lips curved into a wistful smile. "I think you can do whatever you set your mind to, Nora McCall."

Somewhere deep inside her, something clicked into place. Possibilities glowed before her, but the school-board race wasn't foremost in her mind as she accepted Connor's assistance out of their booth.

Chapter Eight

The possibility that she would strangle Connor grew stronger with every passing moment. When Abby had suckered them into concession-stand detail for her Saturday soccer game, Nora had had no idea that he would become such a tyrant. Give a man a barbecue fork and he ruled the world.

"Nora, this dog's getting cold."

She whipped out a wrapper, grabbed a bun and held it out. Connor slid the hot dog between its covers.

"That'll be a dollar." After she placed the money in the till, she turned to glare at Connor, which was about all the movement she could muster. With the grill, ice bin and soda fountain, the stand barely had room for two people. His hip brushed hers, sending a shower of tingling pulses through her system.

"You're in my space, Connor."

He jerked his head. "Customer."

A young boy stood on his tiptoes, two dollars crushed in his fist. "A Coke, please."

She scooped a cup of ice.

"Less ice. The boy looks thirsty."

She gritted her teeth, dumped out a few cubes and then pulled the soda spigot. "Here, you go, honey." The child grinned and walked away, carefully carrying his cup.

Connor's arm grazed Nora's abdomen as he wiped away the one droplet of water she'd splashed on the surface of the fountain. A pulse of pleasure shot through her from the brief contact. Her late-night resolutions were no match for daylight and cramped quarters. She wrestled her control into place.

"Back off."

"You're good with kids." The man didn't play fair, delivering a compliment like that, along with a caress across her cheek.

She jerked her face away and leaned against the ice bin. A good chill would do wonders for her racing blood.

"I like them." She rubbed her arms and looked out at the field. She could see the teams gathered in circles on the sidelines. Almost game time.

"Abby will be fine."

"Her knee isn't."

"Doc Sims cleared her, didn't he?"

"Yes, but—"

"No 'buts.' Stop fretting."

Nora shot up. "I'll fret about my daughter whenever I want to, Connor Devlin. I've been doing it for eleven years."

"Customers. And she's *our* daughter."

Two giggling teenage girls wanted a diet soda, a bag

of chips and a long look at Connor. Nora ripped the bags free from the display stand, while Connor pumped the sodas and accepted their money.

"Well, our daughter is playing with a bad knee on a field with more potholes than the freeway after a long, icy winter."

Connor braced his elbows on the counter and nodded. "Can't argue with that. This is where we used to play touch football every Sunday afternoon. The field was dilapidated then and it's a wreck now."

"It hasn't been resurfaced in ages. The school's budget doesn't extend to the practice lots. The school spends what it has on maintaining the stadium field and makes do with patching this lot. But some of those quickie patches may hide deep holes. I worry every game that Abby or one of her friends is going to hurt herself."

The crowd rose on the rickety stands and cheered as the girls ran out. Despite her worry, Nora smiled as she watched Abby's ponytail sway while she lined up with her teammates.

Connor elbowed her. "Their uniforms aren't very uniform."

She nodded. "The team hasn't had a corporate sponsor this season, so new members weren't equipped with shirts. It's all I can do to keep Abby's old one clean from game to game."

"Why isn't something being done, like a fundraiser? God knows, we did enough car washes in our day." He winked. "I remember one drive was to raise money for some very nice cheerleading outfits."

"You mean those glorified leotards."

"All the better to show off the girls' tremendous athletic ability." Connor waggled his brows.

"Humph," Nora sniffed before she smiled at the frazzled mother approaching with a baby kicking up a fuss and a red-faced boy dragging at her hand.

"Hi, Nora. One hot dog, please."

She almost didn't pry open the roll in time for Connor's fork steaming wiener.

"Here you go, Margaret. That'll be one dollar. Condiments are on the side."

The woman blew a strand of hair out of her face. "Nora, can you grab my purse and take out the money?"

Connor nudged her for the hundredth time in thirty minutes. "Nora, she's got her hands full. Put the toppings on for her. You've got plenty in those bottles."

Margaret beamed. "Why, how sweet of you. No ketchup, very little mustard and relish."

Connor waved his fork like a scepter. "It's nothing. What are neighbors for?

Nora, make that light on the mustard and relish."

"I've got an even better idea."

She smiled sweetly. "Why don't you give Margaret a break and hold the baby for her a while?"

"If you wouldn't mind. Her name's Kelly."

"Not at all." Nora reached over the counter, gently lifted the infant over the counter and then thrust him into Connor's arms. His stunned expression as he stared at the squirming baby was a Kodak moment. For once he had nothing to say.

Nora hummed as she squirted on the toppings and spread them with a knife. "Here you go."

"Thank you. Margaret handed the hot dog to her older son.

"Nora," Connor leaned close to her ear.

"Yes?" She expected him to plead with her to take the baby.

"That was our song you were singing just now." Nora's mouth snapped shut.

"Connor, I can take Kelly now," Margaret said.

He handed the baby over, but not before planting a kiss on top of the child's fuzzy hair. A sense of loss swept over Nora at the sight of him being tender with the baby. He would have been like that with Abby.

"By the way, Nora—" Margaret expertly secured the baby "—I never got a chance to thank you for fighting the annexation. Our house property value would have shot sky-high, along with the taxes. Joe and I worried about having to move."

Connor rested his elbows on the counter and leaned forward. "That's why I'm writing Nora's name in for school board on election day. We need more people who are concerned about the future of our children."

Margaret looked uncomfortable, but her bright gaze was curious. "I've heard a rumor about you two."

"That I'm Abby's father?" Connor's posture was so relaxed Nora could have sworn he was swapping baseball scores rather than facing the community grapevine. Three new customers now circled the stand, and they weren't impatient to be served. "You heard correct. As the father of a terrific girl, I want the best for her education, and I think her mother will fight for all the kids."

"Why isn't your name on the ballot?" Margaret asked Nora.

Flashing Connor a glance that could shred bark at twenty paces, Nora muttered, "Oh, Margaret. It was something I mentioned in passing. It's too late to file."

The man standing behind Margaret stepped forward.

Nora recognized him as one of the recent migrant sub-
urbanites from Columbus; Howard something or other,
she recalled. "Why not do as Connor said, Nora? Be
a write-in candidate. It's about time we had fresh blood
on the board."

"Nora's pledging to lead a fund-raiser for a new
field and uniforms," Connor drawled.

If the man didn't shut up in two seconds, he was
going to have a hot dog stuffed in his mouth, Nora
decided.

"About time! Count me in." Howard pushed his
baseball cap back on his head. "How much do you
figure it would cost to replace the field?"

"I haven't had a chance to investigate it," she ad-
mitted.

Howard rubbed his chin, his eyes thoughtful. "Connor, you're in the business. Can you give us an esti-
mate?"

"My husband is a salesman for Sinclair's Used
Cars," Margaret broke in. "I could have him ask about
sponsoring the team's uniforms." She looked expectantly at Nora.

Biting her lip, Nora gazed at her daughter, who was
hand in hand with her teammates for the pre-game huddle The improvements should be done, could be done.
Someone only had to organize the drive.

Why not her?

"We'll need a series of fund-raisers. With such a
small property base, the school district doesn't have a
penny to spare," she mused aloud.

"What's this?" The glacial tones parted the crowd.
Pastor Devlin, along with her faithful shadow, Wilbur
Ames, appeared before the stand.

"Pastor." This time Nora didn't mind the sudden

press of Connor's body against hers. His warmth enveloped her, protected her. "We were talking about organizing fund-raisers for a new playing field."

Sheila's brow arched. "Oh, really. Truly commendable thought, but the school has needs much greater than a field. However, I'll convey your concern to the board." She turned, dismissing Nora as if she was a nuisance.

Connor's arm circled Nora's waist, and she leaned into the comfort he offered.

"Sounds more like you plan to bury the project, Mother."

Sheila swung around. A faint flush crept across her face, but her condescending smile sharpened as she studied the pair. "The school board's annual agenda is already set, but I'm sure Nora's suggestion can be squeezed onto next year's."

Wilbur hooked his thumbs under his yellow suspenders and spoke in a raised voice to the throng, which had increased in size. "Folks, Pastor Devlin's right. We would all like to have better facilities for our teams, but we simply don't have the money."

"Now, Wilbur, it's not as bad as you think. I'll get the sod at cost and donate the labor to lay it." Connor winked at Nora.

Both Pastor Devlin and Ames looked thunderstruck. An elderly man who owned the local hardware store cupped his hands and hollered, "Connor, I'll donate the paint for the lines."

Another woman called out, "Nora, we could have a bake sale."

The din grew as person after person volunteered. Pride flowed through Nora. She reached down and gripped Connor's hand. He linked his fingers with hers.

They were going to build a new field for their daughter.

Late that afternoon, Nora worked at the desk tucked in the corner of her bedroom. She had at least one hour of peace and quiet before Abby was due home from her victory celebration at the local ice-cream parlor. Spread across the top of her desk was the Miller/Devlin file. If she was going to handle the account, she needed to know the extent of any potential problems.

The sound of a door slamming on the second floor startled her. Both Christina and Eve were at the pottery shop, which didn't close until five. Nora rose, crossed to her doorway and checked the corridor. Abby's door was shut.

What on earth? She walked down the hallway and knocked. "Abby?"

No response. Alarmed, she opened the door and entered. "Abby, are you all right?"

Her daughter lay sprawled across her candy-pink comforter, her face buried in a white eyelet pillow. Nora sat on the bed and stroked the back of Abby's head. "Is your knee hurting?"

"No."

"Have a fight with one of your friends?"

"No."

Nora's hand paused in midstroke. "Did one of the kids tease you?"

"No."

"Want to tell me why you're inhaling that pillow?"

This time Abby's no was half-strangled.

"Are you going to make me play twenty questions all night?"

"Are you going to play lawyer all night?"

"Abigail McCall, that's enough. Get your face out of the pillow before it becomes permanently imprinted and tell me what's wrong."

Abby rolled over, but away from Nora. Tears filled her red puffy eyes. "He can't come."

Nora prayed for patience. "Who can't come?"

"Connor."

A small knot of anger formed in her chest. He had made her daughter cry. "What can't he come to?"

"This Thursday is Parents' Day so I invited him to come."

The knot turned and twisted. Nora had always accompanied her child on Parents' Day.

"I thought the two of you could come together." Nora's tinge of jealousy eased. "But Connor said he had to be out of town. Something about a closing."

Closing. Nora recalled the folders on her desk. A real estate closing. She pulled a tissue from the bedside container and mopped Abby's face. "I won't promise you anything, but I'll talk to Connor. We'll see if we can't work something out."

Abby sniffed. "Okay."

She rose. "Honey, take it easy and rest that knee for a while. I'll see you later."

"Thanks, Mom."

Back inside her room, Nora sat at her desk and pawed through the files. There it was, with its neatly printed green-and-white label: Illinois Franchise Contract. She flipped open the folder and scanned the first page. Her temples began to throb. She tossed it aside and picked up another folder. She thumbed through contract after contract. Methodically she lined up the documents and slapped the file shut.

Rising, she pulled off her red shawl-collar sweater and snatched her jacket. She grabbed her briefcase and shoved the real-estate folder inside.

After all, a prosecutor needed evidence to present her case before revoking the privileges of the condemned man.

Connor whistled as he unloaded a new shipment. After an hour spent on the phone rearranging his schedule, he could relax. His right-hand man in Florida agreed to cover the formalities in Illinois this Thursday, leaving Connor free to attend Abby's school event.

His first as a father.

He opened another bundle. To his delight, a few of the Century Two roses shipped from his Florida operation were budding. He touched the tightly folded petals, which only hinted at the rich pink blossom to come. He would plant them in attractive containers at the front of the greenhouse.

Connor's breath caught as he tore free the packaging on the next batch. Deep-red ruffled blossoms sprung clear on one bush, along with an alluring lavish scent. God, he loved the classics, and nothing was more tried-and-true than Mister Lincoln—the finest red hybrid tea ever developed. Reverently he touched one of the glossy dark-green leaves.

The impromptu fund-raising committee was meeting tomorrow afternoon at the pottery shop. This bloom would look good in Nora's lapel. He lowered his head and inhaled deeply. Magnificent.

Just as breathtaking as Nora.

Thoughtfully he stroked the velvety petals. It was a shame that he would be in a room full of people. Otherwise, he could find some interesting things to do with

Nora and the rose. Even thinking about their kiss the other night caused a swift tightening in his groin. He had awakened that morning aching for Nora, only to spend the afternoon alone in a space no bigger than a tin can. At this rate, he was going to spend the rest of his life in a semi-aroused state.

He needed to figure out ways to alleviate the problem…and soon. The trick was to get past all the thorns shielding Nora.

"Connor! Are you out here?" Nora's yell echoed through the vast greenhouse.

He sighed. Sounded as if she'd grown a few more thorns since he'd left her an hour ago. He put down his clippers and rose from his stool. "Back here," he called, wiping his hands on a rag. He lost any attempt at a welcoming expression when he spotted her face. The temper glittering in her eyes could spark a fire. Clearly she was on the attack and he was the intended bull's-eye.

Since she didn't appear to be in a touching mood, he slid his hands into his jean pockets. Connor forced a casual smile. "This is a surprise. I wasn't expecting to see you until—"

Nora marched across the remaining distance between them and jabbed her finger into his chest. In her other hand she brandished a folder. "It wasn't enough for you to return as the 'Bad Boy Made Good.' You had to make your comeback complete by hooking up with the old flame, enthralling her daughter and then dumping them both. You only told Abby a half-truth about being out of town. When did you plan to tell her you were leaving for good?"

Connor freed his hands and snared hers before she could gouge a hole in his chest. He wrapped her arm behind her back and jerked her body against his. "What are you talking about?"

"It doesn't matter about me. I survived your leaving me before and I can do it again. But what about Abby? She's just a kid. The kittens, the farm, the outings— they're all links in a bond you've forged with her. She's starting to accept you as her father." With sweat beading on her brow, Nora struggled to break his grip. "How could you reject her like that? She invited you to Parents' Day and you brushed her gesture aside like a gnat."

Connor tightened his hold. Her eyes were fierce and bright. The blaze of her saccharine smile was all the forewarning he needed. As her foot raised to crush his, he tried to sidestep, but his legs tangled with hers. Both lost their balance. Twisting to take the brunt of the fall, he grunted from the force of the impact.

Immediately he rolled over, lying on top of her. With one hand, he cuffed her wrists above her head. Battling back his temper, he lowered his face toward hers. "What the hell is wrong with you, Nora? What brought on this tirade?"

She struggled to throw him off. "I saw the documents, Connor. I know."

Ed Miller had taught him to count to ten to keep control; he needed every number before he could speak without yelling. "You know what?" he bit out.

"That you're planning to open a business in Illinois, and the closing is Thursday."

Bewilderment tempered his anger. "So? I'm also expanding Primal Rose to three other states. I would think the news would make you happy. It sure made Barnett delirious with the vision of legal fees dancing through his head."

Nora lay motionless. "You're not moving to Illinois?"

The storm within him dissipated. Suddenly her tantrum made sense. She thought he was going to leave town again. He studied her face and saw the raw pain in her eyes. What would it take for her to believe in him once more? How could he win back her trust?

He brushed his lips gently across hers. "No. The CEO of a national chain can basically live wherever he wants to. And I've decided to sink my roots here."

Nora took a quick sharp breath. "You have?"

Connor trailed a few more kisses across her cheek. Into the void left by anger, desire surged thick and hot. He shifted until her hips cradled his arousal. Her body shivered in response, and lust speared through his system. He found her earlobe and bit it gently.

Tension eased from her body. She made a sound, half sigh, half whimper. "You're not leaving."

"I'm not leaving either you or Abby."

At the restless movement of her hips, raw need whipped through him, driving him to the flash point. The primal smell of the conservatory only fueled his desire.

He struggled to find the slippery leash on his control. Harsh handling could bruise the delicate blossom of trust. He leveraged his upper body away, intending to roll off her.

Her arms circled his neck, yanked him down. "Oh, really? Sure feels like you're in hurry to go somewhere."

Connor looked into her eyes, misty with passion, and heard the snap of his chain.

His mouth crushed hers, powerfully, possessively. His tongue probed, penetrated her mouth. Deeper and deeper, he kissed her as if he wanted to fuse her to him forever. In the perimeter of his fogged vision, he spied a splash of red. He reached out and grabbed the rose.

With a single-handed grip on Nora's wrists, Connor laid the blossom on her chest. Nora raised her head to look at the flower. "What are you doing?"

Connor merely lowered his mouth to sip at the sweet expanse of skin along the line of her neck. She trembled. Smiling, he continued to the first button of her blouse. Her jacket had fallen open during their tussle. He released her hands long enough to shuck it off. When she tried to put her arms around his neck, he again stretched them above her head.

Nora stirred restlessly. "Connor, you're making me nervous."

"Hush," he ordered. "Trust me." If he could get her to believe in him on this one level, maybe she would be able to trust him on others.

He opened the first button, exposing the first hint of the swell of her breasts. Slowly he stroked her skin with the tips of the rose petals. The corner of his mouth turned up when he saw goose bumps rise. His mouth replaced the rose, caressing every inch. Nora shuddered, her eyes drifting closed.

Clamping down on his own raging need, Connor tackled the next button, and the next. First the rose, and then his mouth. "Your skin is softer than any petal," he whispered against the smooth valley between her breasts.

When there were no more buttons, he slid the shirt from her shoulders. This time, she made no effort to move her arms. Her upper body was a quivering bow of damp flesh.

"You're so damn beautiful."

He held the rose over one breast and fanned the bud back and forth across the nipple until it puckered and turned pink. When he finally began to suckle, the need began to burn inside him. Still, he moved to her other breast, tormenting it with the blossom and then drawing the nipple deep into his mouth.

Nora writhed. "Connor, please. I can't take this!"

He surged up to kiss her again, nipping her lower lip. "Oh, no, honey. You're going to stand a lot more before we're done."

Quickly he shed his clothes and removed the rest of Nora's. After settling once more over her, he resumed his gentle torture with the rose. He trailed the petals through the valley between her breasts, along her trembling abdomen, across the soft curls at the juncture of her thighs, stroking until he touched her intimately with the flower. When she cried out, he laid his palm on her stomach to hold her still. He drew the rose across her sensitive folds once more and then held it to his nose.

The essence of Nora, all hot and womanly.

"Connor, please."

He looked up and saw her holding her arms out to him. His control fractured, and he rose to brace his body on his arms. Although his need was raging, he wanted one more thing.

"Nora, look at me," he commanded. Her eyes, smoky with passion, slowly opened. He ripped a petal from the rose and lowered his mouth to hers. In silent invitation he waited. She parted her lips, and he slid the petal into the warm recess. Her eyes widened, and he knew that she tasted herself on the petal. She swallowed heavily. Connor held her face between his hands and kissed deeply, drinking the erotic sweetness of Nora and the rose. He broke off, his gaze holding hers.

"You belong to me." He drove in with one long thrust. She lifted herself, wrapping her legs around him. Together they moved in a timeless rhythm. When she began to climax, he finally yielded to his searing need.

Chapter Nine

Pleasure rolled over Nora as she clung to Connor. The elemental scents of earth and sex perfumed the humid air.

Shifting, she snuggled closer to rub her cheek across his crisp tickling hair.

His chest shook beneath her, rumbled with deep laughter. "Easy, sweetheart. You're close to the family jewels."

She froze, but not before her thigh brushed Connor's semi-aroused manhood.

"Uh-oh. Now you've done it."

He wanted her again. Exhilaration rushed through her.

She crossed her arms on his chest, propped up her chin and met his amused gaze.

He trailed his hand along her side. Every inch of her

skin tingled, trembled with awareness, sensitized to his slightest touch.

If she could imprint this moment on her heart forever, she would. Live on this glorious feeling of freedom. No pressures, no worries.

"Want to move to the house?" Connor cupped and kneaded her buttock.

"Hmm, why?"

"I was just thinking." His chuckle nearly knocked off her delicious perch. "We've never done it in bed."

Unless her imagination was running amuck, his flesh just heated up another degree. She closed her eyes in contentment. "Why be conventional? I wouldn't know what to do in a bed."

"Why?" His breath feathered her face. "Didn't your boyfriends know how to treat a lady?"

He was only a kiss away. Anticipation coiled inside her; she could think only of the coming pleasure.

"I've never slept with anyone else."

The admission quivered in the air, but it was too late for her to snatch it back.

Underneath her, Conner went from relaxed to full alert.

"You mean there's been *no* one?"

She tried to slide off.

He gripped her waist, preventing her escape. "Nora, tell me." His eyes bore into hers.

Reluctantly she released the one truth.

"I've been with only one man, Connor. You. That's it. Now, are you satisfied?"

His hold slackened and she used the opportunity to break away. She stood and grabbed her shirt.

It was so unlike her to expose her emotions, to open herself up. No way would she tell Connor that she had remained celibate because she loved only him. Still loved him after all these years, despite everything she had gone through. She quickly slipped her pants on.

"Why?" Connor, unconcerned with his nudity, stood up.

She forced a light tone. "A single mother with a baby isn't exactly prime dating material, Connor." She tugged on the zipper. "First, I had to contend with the pregnancy and morning sickness, then with school. How I could have made it through college and then law school without Aunt Abigail and my sisters, I don't know. Most of the time, I had to get by on three hours' sleep in order to study, even with their help."

She tried to fasten her shirt, but several buttons were missing. She settled for tying the tails into a knot. The blouse gaped at the top.

"For a long time dating was at the bottom of my list. Then Abigail fell ill, and we took over the shop. There's simply not enough time in the day."

She wouldn't tell him about all the times she rebuffed looks and fielded comments by men, confident that she was an easy mark because she was an unwed mother. Why mention the years she had been ostracized by her own community? Or his mother's snide sermons about the sins of the flesh? Each off-color remark, each indecent look, each improper act had added another link to her suit of armor against vulnerability. She would not yield to it now.

"I'll make it up to you." Connor came over and gripped her shoulders.

"Marry me."

Her worst nightmare had come true. A proposal from the man she loved—not out of love, but out of obligation.

"No, thank you." She lifted her chin.

"Why not? We have a beautiful daughter who deserves both parents in her life."

"She already has me. And if you choose to remain here, she'll have you, as well."

He released her and dragged his hand through his hair. "Abby deserves better."

"Agreed, but life isn't perfect. Abby learned long ago to accept that. She's well-adjusted, happy and doing fine. I don't intend to upset that with a marriage of convenience."

"What about this?" He waved his hand at where they had lain. "What about us?"

Her heart beat a little faster. "There is no 'us.' We made love. It was nice." At his glowering look, she hastened to add, "All right, it was more than nice. The point is, we're both adults and old enough not to let our physical needs control our minds."

"You're too passionate a woman to ignore that side of yourself for the rest of your life."

As Nora slid her feet into her loafers, she realized she had never felt so out of control.

"What about our future?" he asked.

Accept a loveless marriage? No way would she subject herself to an emotional prison like the one she had experienced with her mother. She wanted it all. She and Abby deserved nothing less.

However, there *was* passion, perhaps a base from which love could be built. She and Connor had come so far, so fast; maybe they could have a chance for a future together.

"What about slowing this down, Connor? You've been gone twelve long years and you've only been back one short week."

"Are you going to hold my leaving over my head for the rest of our lives? Are you ever going to forgive me? You don't understand...."

"I understood why you had to go, Connor. I accepted it a long time ago. This isn't about us, it's about Abby."

"But—" A phone pealing interrupted Connor. He strode over and grabbed the portable phone resting on the workbench. "Devlin here." His face lost its angry lines. "Sure, Christina, she's right here." He held out the phone.

Nora took it. "Hi, Christina, what's up?"

"Nora, did you give Abby permission to go out tonight?"

Nora glanced at her watch. It was already after eight. Where had the time gone?

"No." Unease began to stir in her stomach. "Why? Isn't she in her room?"

"No, and I've looked everywhere, including the shop. She's not here. There's makeup out in her bathroom, and her new dress is missing. I thought maybe you changed your mind about her going to the party."

"No, I didn't. I'll go there right now." Nora hit the disconnect button. The Chadwick house was on the other side of town.

She weighed her options and looked at Connor. "Get dressed. I need you to drive me to a house where Abby, contrary to my wishes, is at an unsupervised party with boys."

Connor reached for his pants. "How bad is it that she's at this party?"

"The Chadwicks keep a well-stocked cabinet of liquor and the kids invited include high-schoolers."

Nora cleared her throat and delivered her clincher.

"Remember what you were like as a teenage boy around girls?"

"Endless raging hormones." He tugged on his T-shirt and grabbed his car keys from the bench. "Let's go."

Being cool was hard, maybe even a little bit scary. When Abby had first arrived at the party, everything had been fun. Girls clustered on one side of the living room, talking about the boys, while the boys stood on the other side, talking about the girls.

Abby's heart still raced whenever she recalled how she had slipped out the back door while Eve and Christina watched a movie in the living room. She didn't know where her mom was, but with any luck Abby'd be back home in bed before Nora's nighttime check.

Abby glanced at her watch and gulped. Almost nine. Maybe she should leave before the party got any rowdier.

If only Tony had gotten here sooner.

Initially the kids had been drinking sodas. But then Joe Matuzak, a tenth-grade linebacker, had emptied the contents of the liquor cabinet into their glasses. Now the volume of noise was louder and the partyers began to huddle as couples. In one corner, boy-girl teams competed in a game of Twister. A shriek drew Abby's attention. A varsity cheerleader sprawled on the game sheet with a football player on top of her.

Abby's fingers tightened around her cup of lukewarm Coke. She sought out Tony in the crowd and found him encircled by several older girls. Her pulse skittered at the sight of him. One girl ran her hand along Tony's forearm, and he winked at her.

All of Abby's hopes vanished. No point staying for further humiliation.

She flashed a thin smile at her friends. "Sorry, but I have to go."

A boy with a slurred voice spoke behind her. "Whazza matter, Abby? Your mom's leash not long enough?"

She spun and looked up into Chuck Partridge's leering face. He raised his beer and polished it off. "We haven't had our turn at Twister yet."

Not if he was the last boy in Arcadia. "No, thanks."

He plopped the bottle down, heedless of the coasters scattered about the room. Abby cringed as moisture dribbled from the glass container onto the beautiful oak cocktail table.

He grabbed her arm, his stubby fingers digging into her flesh. "Come on. Let's have some fun."

Panic stirred, but she dug in her heels. "Let go of me!"

However, Chuck was a head taller and a good fifty pounds heavier than Abby. Without effort, he dragged her forward. Abby cast around desperately for a way out.

"Let go of her, Chuck." Tony, his hands on his hips, blocked the other boy's path.

Chuck sneered. "What you going to do 'bout it, Gennaro?"

Although Tony was taller, his lean wiry build made him look vulnerable next to Chuck's stocky solid frame. He took a step closer. "There are plenty of other girls here, Partridge. Pick on one closer to your own age."

Chuck's fingers dug in deeper, and Abby gasped with pain.

Tony's eyes narrowed. "Let her go."

Joyce Chadwick hurried over. "Hey, you're ruining the party." She grabbed Chuck's arm. "My parents will have a cow if anything is broken. Come on. I know where Dad hides his prized scotch."

After a glare at Tony, Chuck shrugged and released Abby. "Here, you can have her. She's still in elementary school, anyway."

After he and Joyce left, Abby fought to suppress a shiver.

"Are you all right?" Tony asked roughly.

"Yeah. Thanks."

"Where's your jacket?"

"In the other room."

"Get it. I'm taking you home."

A hush fell across the room. Abby realized everyone was staring at her. She looked around, saw Nora and Connor in the hallway and groaned. Her mother's face was pinched with anger. "Never mind, Tony. I've been busted."

She knew better than to pray her mother wouldn't make a scene.

However, Connor spoke first. "Hey, Abby. Sorry to drag you away so early, but we have to go." As he walked toward her, the silent group parted. He halted before Tony. Although her father's voice was low, his eyes blazed with suspicion. "Is everything okay?"

Tony shrugged. "Everything's cool. I was about to walk Abby home."

Connor studied both their faces for a moment, then nodded. "Thanks. Don't forget to stop by my place on Monday."

With a studied nonchalance, Tony shrugged. "Sure."

After taking a few deep breaths to steel herself, Abby approached her mother. "Men," she muttered.

Nora glanced at her and smiled sweetly. "Yes, and you'll have plenty of time to think about them."

Abby flipped up her collar and sighed. She was in for it now.

Connor sat on the rickety swing on the McCalls' front porch. For the few moments that he had stood inside, it had been all warmth and confusion. After a hasty greeting, Eve and Christina had demanded an accounting from Abby. Afterward Nora had swept Abby upstairs for a mother-daughter talk. Although the sisters had invited him into the kitchen, he had sought refuge outside.

The squeaking of the swing's rusty hinges was the only sound in the still night. Connor waited, pushing back and forth to release the aftershocks from the day. Next visit he would bring a can of silicon spray.

How much had he been deceiving himself that he could make a go of this ready-made family? Did he think he could play the rescuing knight on his white steed? Did he imagine that he could make everything all right with a snap of his fingers, live happily ever after with Abby and Nora? Given tonight's events, he was clearly out of his depth.

Connor took a deep breath.

His grand homecoming scheme hadn't included winning over a young girl. When it came to having children of his own, Connor had expected to go through diapers and late-night bottle feedings first. Instead he had been dropped into the advanced psychological warfare of a willful teenager.

He hadn't dealt with his own adolescence that well. Only Ed Miller had steered him from a path of disaster.

Just as well Nora had taken on the first round of speaking to Abby. The only person he had had as a model of parental behavior was Sheila Devlin. What a joke.

Sickened by sour memories, Connor closed his eyes and inhaled slowly. The crisp chill air cleansed his mind.

No, he realized. He was wrong about having no role in this family crisis. Any discussion about teenage boys should include him. If Abby's ashen face was any indication, something had happened at the party to upset her before her parents had arrived.

A square of strong light fell across the stoop. Nora stepped out and sat beside him, wrapping her jacket tightly around her.

He draped his arm around her shoulders, silently offering shelter. To his surprise, she shifted closer, fitting into the curve of his body.

"How's Abby?"

"Contrite now that I've grounded her. I just haven't decided for how long. My first inclination was until she's eighteen, but I might be overreacting." She smiled slightly.

His fingers touched her nape and began to knead the tense muscles. "Tough talk, huh?"

"Yes. It's a fine line between telling your child what she should know versus letting her learn from her own experience. You want so much to prevent the hurt, yet at the same time you realize a child must experience life in order to grow."

"You've done fine, Nora. Abby is a great kid. You

remember how it was at that age, on the outside looking in.''

She twisted to peer at his face. "I know I felt that way, but I never realized you experienced the same thing. You always hung out with plenty of boys."

"Sure." He shrugged. "I had the friends I wanted, but I was never considered 'in.' I was the class rebel."

"Never seemed to stop the girls from drooling."

"Except for the one I wanted." He squeezed her neck.

She squirmed.

A woman came into sight, pulled along by her anxious Pekingese. Nora lifted a hand. "Good evening, Mrs. Broten."

"Evening, Nora." The woman included Connor in her smile.

"Looks like Samson's raring to go."

Mrs. Broten laughed. "This air has put an added spring into his step. It looks like it's going to be an early winter."

"I'm afraid you're right."

"Well, Samson has his cozy home in sight. Have fun, you two." The dog led his owner down the street.

Connor stared after her. "I missed this."

"Missed what?"

How to answer the question stumped him. He frowned. "Having neighbors. Knowing the names of the neighbor's dogs."

Nora stared at him in astonishment. "I thought you hated Arcadia Heights."

Connor shrugged. "I sweated out any ill will a long time ago." He was speaking the truth, he realized with surprise. Just now, he hadn't felt like an outsider looking in. Not with Nora by his side.

He gestured at the street. "Look at these homes, all maintained with pride. Very few places have this sense of community."

Amusement glinted in her eyes. "You sound startled. What was it like living in Florida?"

Always uncomfortable talking about his personal life, he glanced at the toes of his scuffed boots. In Florida he had never found the connection he had desperately sought. At first he'd been busy trying to survive from one meager paycheck to the next. Later he'd been absorbed by the demands of starting his own business. But even if he had had the time, he doubted that he could have settled down in the area.

"Oh, it was...different." He looked up. "People came and went, never staying for long. They were either searching for gold or enjoying their last few years of life."

Nora's brows knitted slightly as she studied his face. "Sounds very urban."

He agreed. "It's not Arcadia, anyway. Neighborhoods with families are desolate islands in the midst of retirement condominiums."

"That's sad." Her expression was pensive.

"Yeah, I thought so." Connor surveyed the quiet street. Despite the fact that the town was losing its youth to Columbus, they seemed to have found their way back to Arcadia Heights for the weekend.

Or, like him, they had found their way back home for good. The sense that he had done the right thing by returning to Arcadia Heights solidified within him.

The front door popped open, and Eve stuck out her head. "How about a hand of poker? Nate's here, and we've got beer and popcorn in the kitchen."

Nora laughed. "Sounds like a winning combination.'' She patted Connor on the knee. "Come on. Let's see if you're also a stud at poker.'' She gave him an exaggerated wink.

He rose and offered his hand. "If the stakes are clothes, I'll have you naked by midnight.''

The light revealed her crimson cheeks, but she gave a defiant flip of her hair. "Been there, done that to-day.''

He arched a brow. "Who said you can't do it more than once a day?''

She ducked her head and hurried to the entrance. Connor followed her inside.

Light, warmth and noise engulfed him. He stuck his hands in his pockets and began to whistle as he strolled beside Nora into the heart of the house.

Chapter Ten

Across the street from the church, Nora shifted and leaned against the fender of her car. She glanced at her watch. Any minute church service would be over. Although guilt nipped at Nora for not attending today, the last thing she needed was to face a fire-and-brimstone sermon. She couldn't wait to collect Abby so she could get out of here. No matter how she willed herself not to look, the church once more drew her gaze.

Marry me.

Right words, wrong reasons.

How many times as a teenager had she dreamed of walking out of this church married to Connor? How many times during those anxious months of her pregnancy had she wished he would return to town to proclaim his love and sweep her off down the aisle?

"Be careful what you wish for" was a warning she should have heeded. Somehow her dreams had kept

Connor frozen in time. She hadn't expected, hadn't been prepared for, Connor to return as a grown man.

Every cell of her body still snapped, crackled and popped from the passion he'd awakened with his touch yesterday. A restless night had done nothing to alleviate her state of sensory overload. She hadn't been able to hold a mug without spilling coffee. She hadn't been able to hear the conversation at breakfast because of the blood pumping in her ears. Her stomach felt as if it was tied in one of those Celtic knots Aunt Abigail used to sketch.

How was she supposed to act normal in the midst of mundane weekend tasks when she had experienced the extraordinary?

Never in her wildest dreams had she ever imagined being desired and made love to with such single-minded focus as Connor had last night.

Never had she experienced wanting to the extent that she had experienced it in his arms.

And still, she wanted more. Like a secret kept too long in a dark closet, her desire for Connor finally had been unleashed.

Her emotions were deep, searing in their intensity. Yet, she would have to tread carefully. She felt sure that Connor's marriage proposal had been a knee-jerk reaction born out of passion and possessiveness, not out of love and commitment.

She contemplated the cottage behind the church, where Connor had been raised. With no father and a glacier for a mother, Connor had never known love. Their childhoods had been similar, but Nora had been rescued by Abigail McCall. Could a man who had only known pain at the hands of his mother learn how to trust love? Could he be a loving partner?

People began to stream down the church's front steps. Nora sighed and watched for her daughter. She spotted a few of Abby's classmates, their shoulders hunched, as they silently trailed behind their parents. Abby's posture mirrored her friends' as she approached the car.

Even cinnamon waffles for breakfast hadn't cured her daughter's sulks. Tough. Last night Nora had lost about three lives from worry before she had seen Abby was safe and sound. Maybe during Abby's one-month sentence, Nora might be able to recuperate. However, as she took in Abby's tense expression, she realized something else was afoot.

"What's wrong? Someone miss a note during choir?" she asked lightly.

Abby halted. "Pastor Devlin wants to see you."

"Is there a problem?"

"I don't know." Abby hooked her thumb under a fine chain around her neck. "But she gave me this." A small gold cross glittered in the late-morning light.

"Oh." Uneasy, Nora studied the necklace. Not an overtly expensive present, but given the gift's source, very unexpected. Sheila Devlin had never shown any interest in her granddaughter. Aside from working on the choir together, the two had virtually no contact with each other.

Only one way to find out. She straightened. "It's very nice, honey. Wait here. I won't be long."

Inside she found the minister talking to a few parishioners. Sheila, still wearing her vestments, glanced up and murmured to the others. They left immediately, but not before shooting Nora a curious look as they passed her in the aisle.

Sheila folded her hands in front of her body. "Nora.

Something of an urgent nature concerning you came to my attention this morning, and I felt we should talk.''

"Yes?''

"Last night your daughter was at an unchaperoned party where alcohol was served.''

Nora came to full alert. "Abby, along with *all* her classmates, did attend a party at the Chadwicks'. However, Abby left early.''

"Do you think you're setting a good example by allowing your child to be alone with older boys?''

"That's not what happened.'' Nora clenched her teeth.

Sheila wasn't about to be deterred. A zealous fire lit in her eyes as if she was still in sermon mode. "Oh, I forgot. Your mother was such a bohemian that you probably don't know any better. Your mother tortured your family, didn't she? Her inability to hold a job for more than a few weeks. Her constant begging for money, which she promptly spent on alcohol and drugs. How humiliating it must have been for you.''

The minister's voice rose as if she was preaching to the last pew. "Then there was her promiscuity, which broke her father's heart and put him in his grave. Who could blame Bill McCall for passing on so early? My goodness, such a heavy burden to have a daughter who bore children by three separate men out of wedlock. For a while there was talk that all three men were named Bill—Tess's way of needling her poor father.''

Shame slithered inside Nora's stomach. She jerked up her chin. "We made do, Pastor.''

Sheila favored her with a tight-lipped smile. "You had no choice in the matter. After all, Tess was so busy self-destructing that she abandoned you most of the time, didn't she? Left three young girls to grow up wild and uncontrollable. Of course, being locked up alone in a closet must have been rough on you.''

Like a slap to the face, the taunting words caught Nora off guard. She reeled, fighting to keep her face expressionless before Sheila's raptor gaze. How had this woman found out her darkest secret? Only her sisters and Abigail had known Tess had punished Nora by locking her in a closet, sometimes for days on end. Unless...unless she had gained access to the Child Services' records. With great effort, Nora refocused on Sheila.

''Yes.'' The minister nodded as if she had just had an epiphany. ''I can see how it must be difficult for you girls to not travel down the same path as your mother. Naturally I've tried to help by warning people here to not place too-high expectations on any of you girls.''

''You know nothing about us.''

Sheila's lips thinned with contempt. ''Quite the contrary. I know a great deal about your little family. However, you're the only one who concerns me.'' She paused. ''Your running for the school board flies in the face of all propriety. I want you to withdraw your name.''

Nora folded her arms. ''I'm advocating a new playing field, not the destruction of the school system.''

''The school board is responsible for molding our children.''

''I thought parents were.''

''A school board influences children through its curriculum. We hardly want a mother who is so irresponsible with her own child to serve.''

Nora's temper flared, but she controlled it. ''I am not irresponsible. How can you say that?''

"Easy. For whatever reason you and Connor persist in making a spectacle of yourselves and your high-school indiscretion. It's disgusting and embarrassing. If your disgraceful conduct continues, I'm sure one call to Charlie Barnett will have him reconsider you as an associate."

"Don't you dare insinuate that I'm an incompetent attorney." Nora was incredulous. "Are you threatening my job?"

"I don't need to. Charlie will look at the situation, see the drop-off in his clientele and come to the conclusion that people are avoiding him because of you. If he doesn't, I'll make sure the church withdraws its legal account from him. Surely that won't be necessary, will it? Not after all I've done for your family."

Nora had had enough. "Look, Sheila. I've always been grateful you helped us to secure the second mortgage so Aunt Abigail could stay afloat. But that obligation was paid in full a long time ago.

"Furthermore, I've paid back my obligation to Arcadia Heights, and I continue to do so." She stepped closer to Sheila.

"Heavens, child. You're overreacting. I'm sure others are in a far better position to judge your capability as a lawyer." Sheila's hand covered the large pearl encrusted cross around her neck. Nora recalled Abby's gift.

"Why did you give Abby the necklace?" She couldn't quite strain the grudging suspicious tone from her voice.

"Since I'm now free to acknowledge my grand-daughter, I thought we should become acquainted." Her pronouncement was delivered with cool detachment, as if the minister were advising her of a death in the family. It sent a shiver along Nora's spine. "After all, the poor child needs a stabilizing influence in her life. She's not going to get it from her reckless parents."

An ice pick driven into Nora's back replaced the shiver. "What kind of stabilizing influence?"

"I know the court system hasn't viewed grandparents' rights with favor, but the mortal court isn't the highest one. I can only pray this unfortunate situation doesn't hurt the child."

"Don't you dare threaten Abby."

Sheila's control slipped, and for a brief moment Nora could see an unholy mixture of hatred and revulsion burning in her eyes. However, the minister regained her chilled composure almost immediately. "I can see you're not going to listen to reason. You've just forced my hand in this matter." She reached inside her robe and drew out some papers neatly folded in half. She smoothed them open and handed them to Nora. "Here."

It was a pleading. Puzzled, Nora skipped past the court-case caption and went to the document's title:

Complaint for Child Custody.

Nora's surroundings blurred, faded. She could only hear the rapid beating of her heart. "Comes now the plaintiff Sheila Devlin, by and through her undersigned counsel, and petitions this Court for custody of one Abigail McCall, and as grounds would state..." The words in the next paragraph stood out as if in bolded relief: "Nora McCall and Connor Devlin are unfit parents."

"No." Nora forced herself to breathe, to look up at

her tormentor. "You wouldn't dare. You wouldn't do this to your own son."

"My son is beyond saving."

"This is what I think of your threats." Nora raised her hands, ripped the paper in two and threw the pieces to the floor.

"Such childish behavior, Nora. It doesn't matter. I'm having you served." Sheila formed a steeple with her fingertips.

"What do you want?"

"If Connor leaves town and this disgusting three-ring circus ends, then I'll reconsider suing for custody. However, if you two continue, I'll have no choice in the matter, and I will win. After all, I'm a church minister with a stable community position. I'm also a loving grandmother who has been deprived of her granddaughter all these years because of her mother's wish to keep her dark secret. You, on the other hand, are an unwed mother from an unstable family. You're never home, leaving Abby to run wild. As for my son—" she shrugged "—he's a blight on humanity. I don't think a judge will think twice once evidence is presented."

Nora had spent her life living down her mother's actions. No more. She was her own person.

"You stay away from my daughter. If you so much as look at her the wrong way, I'll slap a restraining order against you so fast it will make your pulpit spin."

"This discussion is over. I'll give you a week to reconsider. If you will excuse me, I have charitable rounds to make this afternoon." With a regal air, Sheila turned and entered the vestry.

Her knees suddenly wobbly, Nora reached out and gripped the top of a pew. She tried to take a few deep

breaths but found the church air too oppressive. Sheila
may have left the nave, but the presence of the sharp
fragrance she wore still lingered. Nora spun on her heel
and sped down the aisle.

Once on the outside stoop, she inhaled the cleansing
fall air. She saw her daughter waiting by the car. The
sun glinted off Abby's hair, bringing out its burnished
highlights. Such a perfect blend of her parents' looks.
Nora knew that her daughter's inner traits also bore the
best of her mother and father. No one would ever be
able to steal that from her child.

Nora took a moment to gather herself, to draw on
her shield of composure before she crossed the street.

"Everything okay?"

She wrapped her arm around her daughter's shoulders. No one was going to take her child away from
her, no one.

"Everything's fine."

"She knows, doesn't she. That's why she gave me
this."

"Yes, she's aware you're her granddaughter." No
sense in telling Abby that her paternal grandmother had
known of her existence three months into Nora's pregnancy.

Nora stifled a groan as she spotted a man walking
toward them. She plastered on a smile. "Good morning, Coach Krinard."

The tall man dressed in a tie and athletic jacket
halted. "Good morning, Abby." He held out his hand.
"Nora, I want to thank you for what you did last
night."

Startled, Nora shook hands with him. "You're welcome."

"If you hadn't called all those parents about the party, I'd hate to think what would have happened."

She shrugged. "I felt it was the right thing to do—" she glanced at her daughter "—even if I'm not Ms. Popular with the kids today."

. The coach laughed. "That's okay. Anyway, thank you again." He nodded and strolled away.

"You squealed on the others?" Abby was aghast.

"Let's just say I used the parents' grapevine system to spread the word."

"Mom!"

"Abby!" She smiled and tugged her daughter's ponytail. "What say we head back home and scare up some lunch?"

"I guess." Abby toyed once more with her necklace. "You think I should get a thank-you card for the minister?"

Nora didn't want to see Sheila thanked for trying to weave her daughter into her destructive web, but it probably would be best to maintain manners for the moment.

"I think that would be appropriate." Thinking of the pristine condition of Sheila's home, Nora smiled grimly. "You could put angel confetti in the envelope."

"Cool."

Fifteen minutes later Nora dropped Abby off at the house and crossed to the rear entrance of the pottery shop. She unlocked the door, stepped inside and flicked on the light. Then she opened a drawer on the kitchen hutch, removed a small box and a tube of ceramic glue, and carried them to one of the worktables.

She carefully laid out pottery fragments. With great deliberation, she sorted them by color and shape like a jigsaw puzzle. When she had two orange-and-black splotched pieces lined up, she applied glue to one edge and pressed them together. She matched another sliver, added a drop of glue, and pressed it against the other two. The moment she eased her grip, all three fragments broke apart.

Abby's special Mother's Day gift had shattered irreparably. It was lost to her forever, as her daughter would be if Nora didn't find a way to stop Sheila. Her hand formed a fist, tightening more and more until blood trickled through her fingers. Nora finally opened her palm and let the red-smeared pieces fall to the table.

The pain from her slashed palm surged and ripped through her numb shock. A sob tore loose, followed by another and another, until her body was convulsed with them. Tears scalded her eyes and coursed down her checks. She leaned forward, buried her face in the crook of her arm and let despair take over.

Connor halted in the shop's rear archway and stared. He had never seen Nora cry. Her anguish washed over him. The urge to comfort her was instinctive, propelling him across the shop.

"Honey, what's wrong?" When she didn't look up, he reached out to gather her close until he saw the bloodstained newspaper covering. Blood still beaded from her curled hand. His heart lurched. "My God, Nora, you're hurt."

He scooped her into his arms. Her stool toppled and hit the floor with a clatter. He carried her over to one of the armchairs in the alcove and tilted her palm to the light. Two shallow cuts flanked one ugly deep puncture wound. "Honey, I have to get you to the clinic. This time I think you've really done it. You're going to need stitches.''

Nora didn't even raise her head from where she had burrowed into his neck. He fashioned a tourniquet with a bandanna and then enfolded her shaking body into his arms. The sobs racking her slender body alarmed him. The force of her crying felt as if it would shatter her into a thousand pieces, like the pottery fragments scattered about the table. He ran his hand up and down her spine while he pressed his cheek against the silken crown of her bowed head.

"It's okay, honey. I know it hurts. Let me get you to the doctor." His gaze fell on the pottery pieces, and his helplessness flared into anger. "Why were you messing with that figurine? It's smashed beyond repair. What's so damn important about it that you're willing to risk cutting your hand again?"

Nora raised her tearstained face. "It's the last piece Abigail worked on with Abby. It was my Mother's Day gift from them."

The anguish in her voice cut him to the quick. He reached for his bandanna and then remembered he'd used it on her hand. He tugged his T-shirt from his waistband and used the hem of it to mop her face. "I'm sorry, honey. I know how important it must have been to you."

Guilt stabbed even deeper when he remembered she had dropped it when she'd seen him on his first visit into town. How on earth was he ever going to make up the loss of the figurine to her?

"Maybe Abby could make you a new cat—"

"No, she can't." Nora wrenched away from him, rising. Temper frosting her eyes, she stood in battle mode, her fists clenched at her sides.

Connor realized that it was sometimes better if a man kept his mouth shut, particularly if he didn't know the first thing about how to comfort a woman. "Look, I'm sorry. I know it could never replace what you lost."

"You're right about that. I can never replace Abby."

He grabbed with both hands for his patience. "I wasn't talking about Abby."

"I was. Your mother threatened me this morning."

"Threats are an art form to Sheila." He rose and cupped Nora's chin. "Tell me what she said to upset you."

"She's suing for custody of Abby."

Whatever he had expected Nora to say, it wasn't this. Her words blindsided him. He didn't think that even his mother could stoop so low. "We'll fight her."

Nora's mouth trembled. "How?"

He saw the naked terror darkening her eyes. "We'll get an attorney and—" he inhaled deeply and released a steadying breath "—I'll testify against her if need be." Maybe he could once more protect his woman.

Nora swayed. He caught her and drew her close. "Tell me what happened."

As he listened to her account of her confrontation with his mother, a deep chill gripped him.

"Connor, she gave me a copy of the complaint. It said hateful things about us. That we're unfit parents."

"No one will believe that about you." The community's verdict on him was still out. "She's bluffing."

"How can you be so sure? After all, she's an ordained minister."

"And I'm her son. I've learned at the hands of the master how to play the same game. Let me see the complaint."

"I ripped it up."

How he wished he could have been there. His mother thinking she had delivered a crushing blow, and his warrior princess defiantly tearing the paper. He hooted with laughter. "Way to go, honey." He lifted and swung her in a circle.

"Put me down!" Nora slapped his shoulder with her uninjured palm.

Instantly contrite, he lowered her. "What's the matter? Did I bump your hand? I'm sorry. I wasn't thinking."

She broke free of his embrace. "And that's exactly your problem, Connor Devlin. You never stop to think about others and their feelings." She paced in front of the fireplace. "What I did was stupid. I shouldn't have done it. Our daughter is in danger, and all you can think about is getting even with Sheila." She threw up her hands. "How could I ever marry you? You haven't changed a bit. All that has ever mattered to you is waging war with your mother."

She swung to face him, temper glittering diamond bright in her eyes. "Well, here's news for you. This isn't a joke. This is serious. Your mother is threatening to take our child. Are you going to stand and fight with me, or are you going to run like you did twelve years ago?"

With each accusation, Connor's heart ached more. After all he had sacrificed to protect Nora and her sisters, this was his reward. Condescension. He had had enough belittlement from his mother to last a lifetime. He couldn't, wouldn't take it from the woman he loved.

He gripped her upper arms. "Don't be so self-righteous. You're not absolved from blame here. You kept Abby a secret from me for twelve years. I missed everything from her first word to her first step to her first ball game." His fingers bit into her flesh. "You denied me everything. What will it take to convince you I would have stayed if I had known you were pregnant? That I would have found a way to defy Sheila?"

Her somber eyes studied him, as if trying to see deep inside, past all his guards. "Why did you leave town, Connor? I think you owe me the truth. Did your mother threaten you?"

Was it only last night that his life-long dream had been within his grasp? When Nora had given herself to him again? She never would have done it if she hadn't still had feelings for him. With a little more time, he would have been able to make her passion grow until he could convince her to marry him.

But the past had reared up to kick him once more.

"What did she do?"

He released Nora and stepped away. "Sheila's always had her thumb on the pulse of this town. She's well attuned to who's in trouble."

He hadn't realized he had balled his fists until Nora's hand covered one of his. He intertwined his fingers with hers. She deserved the truth.

"Like a bloodhound, my mother was quick to sniff out our relationship. She confronted me the night..." He cleared his throat. "Well, *the* night."

"The last night we were together, when we made love," Nora said.

He lifted their clasped hands and brushed his lips over her fingers. "Yes."

"She caught me rummaging for my birth certificate in a box in her office closet."

"Why did you do that?"

His smile was rueful. "I had this notion of marrying you."

"Oh, Connor." Nora squeezed his fingers.

He would never forgive himself for that night. He could still feel Sheila's hatred hammering at him. "She was furious. I had used up all my chances as her son. She wanted me out of the house."

Nora's fingers tightened over his.

"I started tossing what I could into a duffel bag." Anger, hurt and panic had roiled in his stomach. At eighteen he hadn't had a lot of options. "I told her Ed would take me in." And he had prayed that his old friend wouldn't let him down.

"She told me that wouldn't do. She wanted me out of town. I laughed, saying she didn't own the entire town."

His mother had smiled then, sending cold fear scampering down his spine. "She told me I was wrong. One word to Mr. Millman, the bank president, would result in the rug being pulled out from under your aunt's financing. Abigail would lose everything, including your two sisters."

He looked down and found the absolution he had been seeking all these long years simmering deep in Nora's eyes. The tension inside him eased. "I had a hundred bucks to my name and only what I could throw into the bag. I knew she would ruin your aunt if I didn't agree to leave town and never contact you again. I swung by Ed's to say goodbye, but he insisted I spend the night. The next morning I hit the road, but not before Ed pressed money into my hand." The old farmer had given him three hundred dollars, a lifeline until he found his first job in the next state.

"You should have told me. You should have said goodbye at least. I would have understood."

The accusation was soft but deadly. "I tried."

Her brows knitted in a frown. "I think I would have recalled seeing you."

He shrugged. "You were still asleep when I came through the woods and stood below your window. I grabbed a handful of pebbles, intending to wake you up. Then I stopped. You had a home, security, while I had nothing to offer. Abigail had always been kind to me, even buying me ice cream when I was a kid watching the other kids at the ice-cream truck."

Nora smiled wistfully. "I never knew she did that."

"Your aunt was a good woman. She didn't deserve to be dragged into my battle with Sheila. None of you did. So I left." Not before he had whispered the words "I love you" into the night air, with a fanciful notion that somehow his declaration would reach her. They had found so much magic together in the night; why wouldn't it work one last time?

It hadn't. He had turned and walked away from the magic of Nora.

Her arms circled his waist and her body pressed against his. She shivered. He wasn't sure if she was seeking or giving comfort. Maybe, just this once, it could run both ways. He enfolded her in his arms, pressed his cheek against the cool silk of her hair and closed his eyes.

Her body trembled again and he ran a soothing hand up and down her back. "It's going to be okay, Nora. We're in this together. I swear she won't take Abby from you."

It was a promise he intended to keep.

Chapter Eleven

"What's going on here?" Eve's voice carried across the room. Nora lifted her face from the crook of Connor's shoulder. Both Eve and Christina hurried toward them. Eve glared at Connor. "Did you hurt her again?"

Nora hastened to intercede. "No, Eve. It's not him, it's his mother." She pressed a kiss to his jaw. "It's always been his mother."

"Huh? Could you repeat that—in English?" Eve folded her arms and tapped her foot.

Christina looked from one to the other before understanding lit her expression. It didn't surprise Nora that her empathetic middle sister had been able to divine the truth.

Now that the hot flash of roiling emotions had faded, Nora felt drained. She wanted to sit down, but realized that the news she needed to deliver was best given standing up. Connor's arm around her tightened. She accepted his support. "Pastor Devlin's threatening to sue for custody of Abby if Connor doesn't leave town."

"What! That's ridiculous." Eve waved her hands.

"She made Connor leave before, didn't she," Christina said as she sat in the other chair before the fireplace. Eve perched on the chair's arm.

Nora nodded. "She found out about us. She threatened to have the financing pulled on Aunt Abigail's studio if he didn't leave. For some reason our dating infuriated her." She frowned. That still puzzled her. It wasn't as if Connor had been a monk. Quite the contrary. His pickup truck in the school parking lot had drawn girls to him like bees to honey.

"Oh, that's so easy." Christina laughed. "It infuriated her because she knew that this time it was serious for Connor. The other girls meant nothing to him. She probably counted on his leaving town after graduation. Your marrying would have been a real wrench in her plans."

"You know, that never occurred to me." Connor's fingers flexed and unflexed at Nora's side. "I'd always wondered what triggered her anger, when she never noticed or seemed to care who I was seeing before."

"How could she keep track when every girl in Arcadia Heights was chasing you?" Nora couldn't help her tart tone.

Connor ran his finger over the tip of her nose. "Is that jealousy I hear? Honey, my reputation was always overblown. I only dated half the girls. Nate dated the other half." He winked.

"Ahem, can we get back to the subject of Sheila?" Eve glowered.

Nora sobered immediately. "Yes, we need to talk.

She could drag you through the mud along with Connor and me.''

Eve frowned. "Let her try. But what about Abby? You're the lawyer. She can't do it, can she?''

"No. Yes.'' Nora huffed a breath to steady herself. "I don't know. There's been a recent movement to increase grandparents' rights. She can drag the family through the courts. This could be rough for all of us. Sheila has information she shouldn't have. She knows about the closet.''

Christina's eyes widened. "How could she know about that?'' she whispered.

"You forget she's a minister,'' Connor interjected. "People confide in her, tell her private matters. What isn't said, she can figure out.''

Eve and Christina glanced at each other, but it was Eve who spoke. "It doesn't matter what she knows, Nora. We'll fight this all the way.''

"Time to go.'' Connor scooped her up into his arms.

"Hey!'' She cried. "What are you doing?''

"You need to see a doctor about that cut. Any war conference about how to handle Sheila can wait.''

"What happened to your hand?'' Eve asked.

"I punctured it on a piece of pottery.''

"Oh, Nora, you weren't trying to repair your Mother's Day gift by yourself, were you?'' Christina shook her head. "I would have helped.''

"What a klutz.''

"Thanks, Eve.'' Nora had to call over her shoulder as Connor began to thread his way through the shop. "Connor, I can walk. It's only my hand. It's over two blocks to the clinic.''

"And that's only blood drenching my bandanna.''

She saw the wide, dark-red blotches and swallowed. "I can still walk."

"Humor me. I'd drive you, but I rode my motorcycle and left it in front of the house."

Eve raced around them and opened the front door. "Let us know how she is and how many stitches she gets. I have the family record of twenty-five, from when I fell from a tree and hit my head." Her worried expression belied her flippant comment.

"Watch over Abby for me," Nora said. "She's supposed to be doing her homework."

Christina came up with her jacket. "Here. Tuck this around her so she doesn't get chilled."

"I'm fine, really." Nora rolled her eyes and then sucked in a breath as the first cold slap of air hit her. She snuggled closer to Connor's warmth.

Even though it was one o'clock on a Sunday and most of the shops along Maple Street were closed, some people were taking a stroll. At their startled glances, Nora groaned but resisted the temptation to bury her face in Connor's shoulder.

"Connor, what's wrong?"

Nora twisted her head when she heard Molly Deutscher's alarmed voice.

"She had an accident. Cut her hand."

"That's awful."

Nora smiled reassuringly. "I'm fine. Connor's taking me to see Dr. Sims to make sure." She would ignore the queasiness swirling in her stomach.

"I'll run ahead and tell the doc so he can be ready."

"There's no need—"

Connor interrupted. "Thanks, Molly. That would be great."

After her friend had scampered off, Nora glared.

"You're making too big a deal of this. I only need a bandage and some antiseptic."

He continued his march down the sidewalk. "What's the matter, honey? Rough, tough attorney scared of a few stitches?"

Stitches. Her stomach churned.

He glanced down and his eyes narrowed. "Interesting shade of green you're turning. You're afraid, aren't you."

She nodded, not willing to risk opening her mouth.

"Don't worry. Doc Sims will give you something to deaden the pain."

She gasped, "That something is usually in the form of a needle."

"Hmm, needle phobia." He shifted her, cuddling her closer. "Speaking of phobias, do you want to tell me about the closet?"

"What?" Nora struggled to control her nausea.

"You said Sheila knew about the closet."

She slowly looked up at him. "You should have been a lawyer. Good questioning technique. Strike with the crucial query when a person's mind is distracted with a minor issue."

Connor's slight smile didn't reach his eyes; they glinted with anger. "Did your mother shut you up? Is that why you've always been afraid of dark closed spaces?"

She sighed. "Part of it was my fault. At first she would simply lock us in our bedroom when she had a man over. As we got older, our presence seemed to unnerve her companions. Without a thought as to whether we had milk or food to eat, Tess would go off for days when she found a new man. Whenever I saw her dressed up, I'd fight with her. She'd drag me into the hallway closet. It might be one or two days before she let me out."

"Why didn't anyone stop her?" Connor stepped off the curb, crossed the alley entrance and continued down the next block.

She pressed her cheek against the cool leather front of his jacket. "Tess moved around too much."

"I could kill her."

Her laugh was bitter. "You're too late."

"What finally happened? I know Child Services brought you to Abigail."

"On the last night we saw Tess alive, she was pulling on her 'going to get me a new man' dress, this clinging black number that left nothing to the imagination. I remember thinking how beautiful she was, with her thick straight black hair, pale skin, blue eyes. But all the while, I knew that my mother was a tramp. The school kids and neighbors all made sure we knew it."

She skimmed her palm beneath his jacket and flattened it against his chest in search of his strength. "Something snapped in me. I screamed at her, saying how disgusting she was. When I saw her face, I knew I had made a bad mistake, but I couldn't snatch the words back. I heard the scraping sounds of the kitchen chairs behind me as Eve and Christina steeled themselves for her reaction.

"I couldn't let them suffer for my mistake, so I threw her last bottle of rum against the wall, all the while hoping she wouldn't hear my knees knocking. It seemed like an eternity before she turned away from the apartment door and slapped her purse down on the end table. The force shook the shade on the lamp so much that the bulb flickered. She stalked toward me.

In the wavering light her expression was wild-eyed. I've never been so scared. I put distance between me and my sisters.''

"She grabbed me by my hair." Hot tears sprang to Nora's eyes, just as they had that night when pain had raked her scalp. "She dragged me into our bedroom." All the way Nora had bitten her lip so that she would not be tempted to beg for forgiveness. It hadn't mattered. Tess had thrown open the closet door and thrust Nora into it. The enclosure had been about the size of a coffin.

"My last words to her before she shut me in were 'I hate you.' She laughed and said she would see how I felt after a night without light." The darkness had pressed all around her as she heard the click of the door lock being turned and then the rap of her mother's heels on the bare wood floor. Moments later the front door banged open.

"My sisters came into the bedroom and scratched on the door."

Eve's frightened voice had carried into the darkness. Seeking to comfort her baby sister, Nora had pressed her cheek against the wood. "It's okay, sweetheart. I'm fine. Christina will take care of you tonight. Tomorrow, Mama will forget all about it and let me out." Swallowing the lump of fear in her throat, Nora had hoped her reassurance would come true. Tess had never beaten the girls, which would have left physical evidence and alerted their teachers, but she had known how to exact punishment in other, invisible, ways.

"I heard a muffled thump and called out to my sisters. Christina answered. They had dragged the mattress off the bed over to the door. She told me I wouldn't be alone—they would watch over me that night. I put my hand on the panel. I didn't have to ask, didn't have to see, to know that my sisters' palms were pressed on the other side of the door. I felt our connection.'' As now she felt the connection to Connor, the steady beat of his heart strangely soothing.

She went on. ''During the night the authorities came and got us. Tess had died from a cocktail of alcohol and drugs served up by an unknown man. The police never found him. And I never could...'' Her voice trailed off.

''You never could recant your last words to your mother.''

''Yes.''

He pressed his face against her temple. ''It wasn't your fault, honey. Some people can't be saved. Your mother was one of them. She chose her own path. Instead of protecting her children, she neglected them. You saved your sisters—focus on that.''

She blinked, nodded.

''Good.'' He halted. ''We're here. Are you ready?''

Nora dabbed her eyes and tucked her hair behind her ears. She circled her arms around his neck. ''Ready.''

The clinic door opened and Molly stood in the doorway. Connor swept her inside. The blast of warm air felt good.

''By the way, honey....''

''Hmm?'' Nora was trying not to think of the needle that was probably waiting for her at the end of the hallway.

''You could stand to lose a few pounds.''

''What!'' She swatted his chest.

Connor's laughter carried them into the examination room.

* * *

Even through the last snip of thread, Nora maintained her composure. Her skin was so translucent Connor swore he could put his hand through her like a ghost. Still, she hadn't complained when the doctor cleaned her wounds and put in a few stitches to close the deepest part of the gash. Only the tremor of the fingers on her good hand, linked with his, had revealed Nora's pain.

He leaned over and brushed his lips across her cheek. "You're almost done, honey."

Doc Sims glanced up, his dark eyes sharp under the overhang of his bushy white brows. "I want you to keep it dry tonight. Change the bandage daily. One of your sisters can help you, can't they?"

"Yes. I'm sure Eve will take great delight in the fact I only have three stitches."

The doctor grunted as he finished wrapping her hand with gauze. "Gotta love her competitive spirit." He straightened, rubbing his back. "But I want you to stay away from pottery until this heals. You and the stuff don't mix. How you managed to cut yourself by only handling it, I'll never know."

She flushed and looked down. "I was upset at the time."

The doctor's gaze turned to Connor. Connor shook his head. "Not me. My mother."

Nora's head shot up. "Connor. No."

There had been too many secrets in his life, he thought, and before them was a man whose opinion mattered in the town. As physician, deacon and school-board member, Doc Sims wielded a lot of influence, perhaps even more than his mother. His decision made, he squeezed her hand and prayed she would go with him.

"Doc, we need your help."

"Well, let's not talk in here, son. Let's go into my office."

Connor assisted Nora off the table.

"What do you think you're doing?" she whispered.

"Trust me."

Files and journals covered the doctor's desk. Books jammed his bookshelves. All other available space contained pictures of townspeople: from beaming mothers holding their babies to young adults holding their diplomas. The doctor settled into his worn leather chair while Nora and Connor sat opposite. He reached into a stand, removed a pipe and held it aloft, his brow arched. They both shook their heads. With a pleased smile, the doctor packed tobacco in the bowl, tamped and then lit it.

"Ah," he said, leaning back. "I don't permit myself many vices, but a quiet Sunday afternoon smoke is one." He puffed a few times while he studied his guests. "What's Sheila up to?"

Nora squirmed, but Connor leaned forward, bracing his elbows on his thighs. "She showed Nora some legal documents this morning. A complaint suing for custody of Abby."

The doctor choked and leaned forward. After a few hacking coughs, he sputtered, "What? Sheila's trying to take Abby away?"

"Yes."

"That's the most harebrained stunt I've ever heard of. Almost beats the time you set off firecrackers during church service."

Warmth crept across Connor's cheeks. "Doc, I was twelve."

The doctor puffed meditatively for a few seconds.

"I never thought it would come to this." He pointed at Nora.

"You've got yourself upset over nothing. A mother's worst nightmare, but the pastor will never succeed. You're a lawyer, get someone to represent you."

He puffed a few more times. "I hear you're going to be a write-in candidate for the school board."

"Yes."

"Opposing the annexation was great. Never told you how proud I was, and how proud Abigail would have been."

He paused and cleared his throat. "I also hear you're organizing a fund-raiser for a new soccer field. That's good." His bushy brows drew together. "I've been on the board for thirty-odd years. Time for fresh blood. Think it's about time I stepped down in favor of someone with new ideas."

Another puff of smoke rose. "Don't you dare withdraw your name for the write-in. I'm announcing my resignation and throwing my support behind you. That oughtta get Sheila's goat. Do her some good to have opposition."

"Your mom's under consideration for a higher post in the ministry."

"So she told me."

The doctor waggled his brows. "We have a meeting at the church tomorrow night at seven. I want you both to be there."

The tension in Connor's chest eased. "We don't know how to thank you—"

The doctor cut him off. "Nonsense. I'm doing what's good for the town."

Connor rose and after hesitating, Nora followed suit.

"Remember. The church tomorrow night."

"We'll be there." He put his hand to Nora's waist as they walked to the door.

"By the way, I expect an invitation."

Connor looked over his shoulder. "An invitation to what, Doc?"

"Your wedding."

Connor couldn't help his grin, although Nora's back couldn't have gotten any more rigid. "You're on the list. As soon as she says yes."

"You may not be finished with telling Dr. Sims everything, but I'm leaving." She thanked the doctor and then sailed out of the room.

The doctor hooted. "My money's on you, son. Go get your woman."

"Yes, sir." He winked and sauntered after her.

Outside, Nora blinked, then rubbed her eyes. With a grin wider than a football field, Eve stood at the curb, leaning against a gleaming motorcycle.

"Eve! What are you doing with Connor's motorcycle? You didn't have permission to ride it."

Her sister gave an unrepentant shrug. "I figured he would need it. After all, he came to the house hoping to take you on a Sunday drive." She reached into her pocket, drew out a knit hat and gloves and tossed them to Nora. "Here, you'll need these."

"I'm not going anywhere."

"Why not?" Connor's arm snaked around her and drew her against his body. "Just think, honey. The wind combing its fingers through your hair, a great throbbing beast between your legs and at your command."

The image his words evoked was not a ride on a

motorcycle, and the irritating man behind her knew it. She knew it, as well, but it didn't stop her from experiencing a tingling rush of expectation.

He nuzzled her neck, sending another shower of desire through her. She hesitated. The sky had cleared; it looked as if it was going to be a gorgeous afternoon. What would a ride through the countryside hurt? She'd never ridden on a bike before. She bit her lip in indecision.

"She's weakening. Come on, honey. Let's go."

"Nora, Connor!" Christina hailed them as she rushed down the sidewalk. Panting slightly, she halted. "I thought you should know. I found a note from Abby. She's gone to take Pastor Devlin a plant to thank her for the necklace."

Connor's body tensed and he dropped his arms. Nora turned around. His eyes were hard and his jaw was set as if he was poised for battle. Her heart began to race. "Connor, what is it? Surely, your mother wouldn't grab Abby and hold her."

"It's not that. It's what Abby is doing. Come on. We have to get over there." He strode toward his bike. Eve flipped him the keys and he caught them in midair without losing a step. He slung on one helmet and held out his hand. Nora hurried over and clambered on behind him. He gave her the other helmet. The motorcycle roared to life, and Connor swung into the street.

Nora yelled to be heard over the engine noise. "Is Abby in danger?"

"I don't know, but I don't want to take a chance."

Clear of traffic, he gunned the engine and the sped up. She clutched him, pressing close. "Please tell me what's wrong. You're scaring me."

His hand covered hers at his waist. "When I was six, Sheila beat me for tracking dirt into church."

"Go faster." Nora closed her eyes and willed them to get there in time.

Chapter Twelve

Abby shifted the potted African violet in her arms and grimaced. A smear of dirt ran down the front of her fire-engine red jacket. Oh, brother. She didn't notice the door to the drugstore swing open; two women hurried out, jostling her. She gasped as the pot slipped free.

"I've got it." Someone snagged the plant.

"Thanks!" She looked up and her knees turned to jelly.

Tony, the plant tucked in the crook of his arm, stood scowling at her. "Next time try watching where you're going."

Despite the chill, Abby felt warmth spreading across her face. "Please give it to me." She put out her hand, but he shook his head. She gritted her teeth. She was tempted to snatch it back, but he was holding it too close to his body. Besides, across the street stood a group of giggling high-school girls. Now was not the time to do anything uncool.

"Fine. You can stand there all day and hold it." She turned on her heel and marched off. When she got home, she'd have to tell Aunt Eve. Eve would high-five her for acting so mature.

Tony caught up and fell into step beside her. "Where are you going with this poor excuse for an African violet?"

Incensed, she kept her gaze forward. "How do you know it's an African violet?"

"Worked with my dad on weekends."

"You mean just playing around in your yard?"

"Construction workers can have hobbies. Pop used to moonlight doing yard work until he got hurt on his day job."

"Oh." Abby cast him a surprised glance. "I'm sorry. Is he all right?"

"I guess. He hurt his back and needed surgery, so he's been out of work." His voice was gruff. "I'm looking for a part-time job until he's back on his feet."

She wasn't sure what to say, but she knew how she would feel if her Mom was hurt. "I'd be scared if something ever happened to my mother."

"Yeah, well, you're a girl."

She rolled her eyes. "And you're a boy. Big deal." Then she had an inspiration. "I've got an idea. Why don't you ask Connor for a job? He's going to need a lot of help." She held her breath. If he worked for Connor, she'd get to see Tony more. Maybe even every day.

Tony stopped and thrust the plant at her. "What is it with you Devlins? Trying to cram a job down my throat every two minutes?"

Dumbfounded by his anger, Abby almost dropped the violet again. With a muttered oath, Tony steadied her hands on the pot. She tightened her grip and he let go.

"What are you talking about?"

"Your dad offered me work already."

Then it struck her. "You called me a Devlin. My last name is McCall."

"Connor's your father, isn't he?"

"Yeah."

"Then you're a Devlin, and you're just as pushy as he is."

"Well, excuse me for trying to help."

She considered the possibility of using her father's last name someday. Would her Mom mind?

Suddenly realizing they had reached the church, she halted at the path to the house. She glared down at the plant and frowned. Maybe the leaves had too many brown spots. She'd been struggling to keep it healthy since Abigail's death. Abigail had been her great-aunt, but in Abby's eyes she'd always been her true grandmother. Now she had a new grandmother, she'd thought it would be cool to give her the violet. However, what had seemed like a good idea in her bedroom didn't seem so hot in the light of day.

She forgot her anger at Tony. "You really think it looks bad?"

"Depends."

"On what?"

Tony's mouth curled into a devilish smile. "Whether you're planning to bury it at the cemetery."

She rolled her eyes. "It's a thank-you present for Pastor Devlin."

His face sobered. "You're kidding, aren't you?"

"She gave me this necklace this morning." She fingered the chain. "Since she's my...grandmother—" it was still hard to think of the minister as being a relative "—I thought I should give her something." She added defensively, "People give flowers and plants all the time."

"Not to the minister." He gestured at the yard. "In case you haven't noticed, she's not into flowers. Dad did the lawn here until he had a fight with her."

She took a step back. This was beginning to look like a really bad idea, but she tried one more protest. "It's for her house."

"Have you ever been inside?"

"No."

"I have, when the minister paid Dad. She doesn't have a plant in the house."

"Oh." She bit her lip.

"Abby." The minister stood in her open doorway. "Were you coming to see me?"

She made a quick decision. Retreat at all costs. "No, ma'am. Tony and I were just talking."

He looked at her but said nothing.

Her grandmother came down the stairs and walked toward her. "Well, it is fortuitous that you stopped here. I have something to discuss with you."

Abby shifted the pot in her arms. She was stuck now. Stopping a few feet away, the minister frowned. "Tony, I wish to speak to my grandchild alone."

Tony shrugged and turned to leave.

"Before you go, take that filthy plant and get rid of it," Sheila added.

"No!" Abby panicked and tightened her hold on it.

Sheila's lips thinned. "I see I have work to do. You have too much of your father in you."

Before Abby could react, her grandmother wrenched the pot from her hands and threw it on the lawn. "When I give you an order, I expect you to obey it."

Abby uttered a small cry and crouched down. She began to scoop the dirt back into the pot.

"You come with me." The minister reached for her. Abby fell on her butt and scrabbled backward to avoid her.

"You leave Abby alone!" Tony rushed up to Sheila and grabbed her arm.

The minister raised her free hand and slapped him. Hard. The sickening sound filled Abby with horror. "Tony!" she cried.

A motorcycle roared along the street and stopped in front of the church.

"Abby!"

She rubbed the back of her hand over her watery eyes and looked around. "Mom."

Nora and Connor ran up the sidewalk. Her mother stopped beside her and dropped to her heels. "Are you all right?"

"She hit Tony!" Abby's lower lip trembled. "I hate her. She'll never be my grandmother."

"You'll change your tune when you're living with me," Sheila said.

Abby gasped. Her mother steadied her while Connor reached down, grabbed their arms and guided them both up. When her mother slid an arm around her, Abby leaned into her. "What's she talking about, Mom?"

The minister folded her hands in front of her body. "I plan to sue for custody of you. It's quite obvious you're picking up your parents' reckless ways. If I don't intervene now, you'll turn out just like your mother.''

A cold sick feeling swept over her. "Mom?''

Her mother ran a soothing hand over her back. "Don't worry, honey. It's not going to happen. She's never going to have you.''

Connor stroked her cheek with his knuckles. "Your mother's right. You have nothing to worry about.''

Tony, who had picked up the ruined violet, stood a few feet away. "Are you okay?'' Connor asked him.

Tony nodded. With a murmur of thanks, Connor took the plant from him. Casting Abby a sympathetic look, Tony moved across the yard to the street. Connor advanced on the minister.

"Looks like we've come full circle, Mother.''

She arched a brow.

Her father held out the plant. "Remember when I made a similar offering?''

Her nostrils flared. "How could I forget such a sacrilege?''

"For God's sake, I was only six years old. I was trying to win your love by bringing you something I cherished.''

"By tracking dirt down the church aisle with that horrid red wagon? By placing a clump of weeds on the altar?'' The minister's disgust coated every brittle word. She hated her own son, Abby realized with horror.

"They were mums.''

"They were garbage and had no place in a church.''

Her father's face was flushed. "As I had no place in your life. You made that real clear the day you hit me.''

Her mother's grip on Abby's waist tightened. "She struck you for bringing a plant into the church?''

Connor's mouth twisted in a mocking smile. "You might say that if it wasn't a slap heard around the world, it was a slap heard across the nave. It certainly set bells ringing in my head for the rest of the day."

A muscle twitched along his jaw. "Your loss of control scared you, didn't it, Sheila? Told the doc I had fallen and hurt myself. After that close call, you were more careful when you hit me physically. Mentally is another story."

He took a pinch of soil from the pot and let it trickle through his fingers. "Stay away from my family, Mother. You come near them and I'll expose you like these grains of dirt." Without waiting for a response, he turned and walked up to Abby and her mom.

His stark gaze fell on her face, and then a smile softened his features. He raised his hand and rubbed his thumb across her cheek. Only then did Abby realize she was crying, crying for that little boy whose gift of love had been rejected long ago. "It'll be all right," he said to her. "I promise. I won't let her hurt you, ever."

He swung his free arm around her mother's shoulders, sandwiching Abby between their bodies. The knot in her stomach eased.

"What say we head home?"

She watched her mother and father look at each other, and suddenly she knew. They still loved each other.

Abby smiled. "How about some hot chocolate, Mom, Dad?"

Before she could take another step, her father bent down and gave her a big smacking kiss on top of her head.

"Dad!" Despite her protest, Abby couldn't help but

grin at the dopey pleased look on his face. Maybe she would take his name when he and Mom got married. Or she could put the last names together with a hyphen. That would be really cool. McCall-Devlin, or would it be Devlin-McCall? She'd have to ask her aunts.

Nora went to work Monday morning, because that was what she was supposed to do. Never mind that worrying about the meeting tonight had caused her to chew through a roll of antacid tablets. Never mind that she had gone to her daughter's room and lain beside her in the early morning hours, unable to sleep.

It was seven o'clock, a workday. And work she would, even though she was screaming inside. She poured herself a mug of coffee and wandered into her office.

Although it was early, she knew her friend would also be in his office and made the call. "Brad?" she asked at the gruff response. "It's Nora McCall."

Brad Preston's voice warmed measurably. "Nora? How are you?"

She hesitated, biting her lip.

"Nora, what's wrong?"

His concern made her decision to be direct. "I have a legal problem. I need your help."

"Shoot."

Her fingers tightened around the receiver. "You knew I wasn't married but had a daughter."

He laughed. "Yes. You were also totally oblivious to the fact that every eligible male in our class had his tongue hanging out over you."

Despite her tension, she smiled. "Sure I did. Those dark circles under my eyes from lack of sleep were a real turn-on."

"You'd be surprised what turns on a male."

Thinking of Connor, she would have to agree. "Apparently. Anyway, the father of my child came back into our lives—"

"Nice of him to reappear after leaving you to fend for yourself for so long."

Brad's automatic defense pleased her, but she hastened to clear the score. "No, Brad. Connor never knew he had a daughter. I had made a bargain in which I agreed to never contact him." She explained the situation to him.

"Nora, how could you?"

"I was young. I thought it was for his own good."

"You thought wrong."

"So I've learned." She took a deep breath. "Anyway, he and Abby have hit it off. I think it's going to work. I think he's going to be a good father to her." She just didn't know if he could also be a loving husband.

"Don't tell me he wants custody of her?"

"No. His mother does."

There was a moment of silence. "Say that again."

"Connor's mother is the person I made the deal with. She's extremely unhappy that her son has returned to town. She's threatened to sue for custody if he doesn't leave. In fact, she's gone so far as to have an attorney draft the complaint. I want you to represent us."

"Did she state any grounds?"

"Yes. We're unfit parents, endangering the welfare of the child."

Another silence. Then Brad's laughter roared over the line, so loud she had to hold the receiver away from her ear. "Brad?"

"Oh, Nora. Thank you for the best laugh I've had all week. And thank you for giving me a case that's a slam-dunk victory."

His confidence was a soothing balm to her raw nerves. "Thank you, Brad."

"Don't mention it. I'll do some preliminary research, but I ought to be able get rid of the complaint on a motion to dismiss. She'll never even get to the merits."

"That's good to hear. I'd rather my family's life not be dragged through open court." Nora's fingers tightened on the receiver. "I think you should know Sheila has a history of violence."

"A pastor?"

"Yes. She hit Connor when he was young, and yesterday she slapped a boy who was trying to protect Abby from her."

"Then the first thing we'll do is get a restraining order. Give me the boy's name in case I need to talk to him."

She gave Brad the information he needed. "Can you get me copies of all our birth certificates?"

"I'll fax a request for them this morning."

She bit her lip. "We'll probably need all Abby's medical records. I can get those from her doctor."

"Where was she born?" Brad asked a few more questions. "This will give me a start. I want you and Connor to compile a list of character witnesses. I'll call you later."

She thanked him again and began to hang up the phone.

"Nora?"

"Yes?"

"I want to meet this Connor. I have to meet the man

who stole your heart so completely that you've never even looked twice at another.''

"You will.'' Nora hung up and turned to face her window. She should call Connor. There was a rap on her door, and she swung around.

Charlie Barnett stood in the doorway. A short man with thinning white hair, he wore his Monday uniform of navy wool suit, white shirt and red-and-navy-striped tie.

"Good morning. Did you have a successful fishing trip?''

"Yes. I did. Thank you.'' He fingered his tie.

"What's wrong, Charlie? You look nervous.''

He huffed, drew in another breath. "I hate to tell you, but we have to get rid of the Devlin account. I have a conflict.''

She rose. "Why?''

"Because we represent the church.''

"Why's that a conflict?''

"There may be some property issues.''

"What issues?'' She stalked around her desk.

"Nothing I can talk about until I make sure of your loyalty.''

"What?''

"In fact, I think it's best to remove you from all church legal work until this blows over.''

The church was their second-largest account. Sheila had been quick to act on another threat. She forced herself to lean against her desk and fold her arms. "Pastor Devlin has talked to you.''

He rotated his head as if his collar was too tight. "Yes. She was kind enough to bring certain matters to my attention. I'm sure it will blow over when her son leaves town, but until then, I'm going to have to put you on part-time. I can't afford to pay you full salary if you're not productive.''

"First I was removed from the account and now I'm part-time? Why don't you come right out and fire me? Wouldn't that be more honest?''

He flushed. "Now, you're overreacting. You've done good work for me. Maybe in a few years I might have made you a partner.''

"In a few years? The last time we talked you were going to offer me a partnership at the end of this year.''

"Well, we'll hold off on that for now.''

She straightened. "No, we won't hold off on it. I won't work for someone who caves into pressure from a client. I quit.'' She walked around and began to jerk open her drawers.

"Aren't you being hasty? I have the only law office in town. You'll have to commute to Columbus every day, something you don't want to do.''

"That was when Abby was younger and I wanted to be nearby.'' She found a plastic bag and emptied a drawer's contents into it. "Besides, who says I'm going to commute? I can open my own office.''

"The hell you can. We have a contract.''

She looked up and smiled sweetly. "I struck through the noncompete clause and you initialed the change.''

"We'll see about that.'' He stormed out of the office.

In the ensuing silence, Nora sank back in her chair and covered her face. What had she done? She couldn't afford to be out of work. There were bills to pay, and the pottery shop needed her occasional cash outlay.

The shop. She spun in her chair and went to the window. She could see its cheery purple shutters. Her gaze settled on the second floor. The empty second floor. She could set up an office there. At least it would be rent-free. With a little advertising in the suburb areas surrounding Columbus, maybe she could pick up enough business.

First things first. She needed to find boxes to pack. She swept out of the office.

Five-fifteen, and Connor's mood couldn't have been fouler. During the brief hiatus from the easement mixup, his work crews seemed to have forgotten where they had left off. He had spent the morning with the supervisors going over the plans. Then, a run into Columbus for supplies had taken more time than expected.

As he pulled into the clearing, the sweep of his headlights caught two other vehicles still parked there in the gathering gloom. Great. What had gone wrong now? He glanced at the dashboard clock again. He had an appointment at seven and he had promised to pick Nora up by six-thirty. He climbed out of his truck and scooped up his bags.

A woman waiting on the porch scurried down the steps toward him. The motion detector light he had installed on the eave blinked on. He recognized Molly Deutscher, her bangs blowing in the harsh wind.

"Connor." She crossed to him and beamed. "Good evening!"

Connor forced his worry back and returned the greeting. "What are you doing here, Molly?" he asked.

"I've come to apply."

Lost, he rubbed his chin. "Apply for what?"

The lively sparkle in her eyes dimmed. "I thought you were hiring…" Her voice trailed off.

Connor was stunned. "You came to apply for a job? With me?" Her husband, Tom, had always made it clear he didn't like him. The feeling had been mutual.

Her face brightening, she nodded. "I heard you were going to have a gardening shop. I'm experienced in sales, Connor."

He braced his hands on his hips. "Does Tom know you're doing this?"

Molly's dark eyes snapped. "No, and it doesn't matter what he thinks. I'm tired of his rehashing old history, and I told him and a few others exactly that yesterday. I need a job. I love meeting people and helping them. I'm perfect for your sales center." A plea softened the anger in her eyes.

Sometimes acceptance came when you were least looking for it. This one was in the form of an earnest young woman, who also happened to be the wife of one of Connor's biggest critics. Considering the situation, Connor rocked back on his heels and laughed. "Well, Molly. I guess I'm just going to have to let you have the job."

She threw her arms around him. "Oh, thank you, Connor!"

Working free of her hug, he said gruffly, "You're welcome. How about our getting together next week to go through catalogs and select merchandise? I also want to feature local work, so maybe you can put together some people willing to sell their crafts through the store."

Molly nearly bounced in her excitement. "Consider it done!" She hurried off to the battered sedan and paused. "Connor, welcome home."

"Thanks, Molly."

Only after her car had driven off did the shadowy figure hovering on the porch detach itself from the railing and walk down the steps. "Mr. Devlin?" Tony stuck out his hand. "You mentioned a job."

Shaking hands, Connor studied the boy. Bronzed skin, steady eyes and firm callused hands. He'd do. "Yes, I did. Interested?"

Tony nodded. "Yes, sir. I'm good with plants. You can ask my dad. I can work weekends and nights."

"What about study time? You're in high school. Aren't you planning to go to college?" Connor prodded.

A raw mixture of pain and pride flashed in the boy's dark eyes, but he replied evenly. "My dad's hurt. We need the money." He hunched his shoulders. "Besides, I'd rather be outdoors than stuck in a classroom."

He had once been in the kid's shoes, Connor reflected. There would be time to work on Tony about continuing his education. It was one thing to work the land; it was quite another to balance the books every night. He knew. He had spent eight long years of night school to get his college degree. "How would you feel about learning the cultivating end of gardening?"

Tony's smile was white against his tanned skin. "I'd feel just fine about it, sir."

"You're hired, on one condition."

Tony dropped his smile. "What's that, sir?"

"Quit calling me 'sir.' The name's Connor."

"Yes, sir…I mean, Connor."

The smile flashed again. This kid was a killer, Connor mused. He would have to watch him around Abby. "Good. Can you report Saturday morning at seven? I need help setting up the main greenhouse. We'll discuss salary and all the other particulars then."

"I'll be here. Thank you…Connor." Tony began to whistle. He turned and walked to the battered black pickup truck in the drive.

Connor waited. When the boy opened the door, he

caught a flash of red. Yep, he was definitely going to keep an eye on Abby. He knew what effect a red leather interior could have on girls.

Justice was exacting her sweet revenge. He would soon experience the same hell as the parents of the girls he'd once dated. The phone rang inside, and he dashed up the stairs, chuckling all the way.

Chapter Thirteen

Tension was rapping a quick percussion set against Nora's temple as Connor parked the truck. Her building headache was the least of her problems. She didn't know what was going to happen tonight, but it would be one more time for public scrutiny. Her family would again be put on display.

Could she count on the silent man who opened the door and assisted her out? He had been positively grim from the moment he had arrived at the house to pick her up. She had taken one look at his remote expression and had sought refuge in her self-containment. She could return cold for chill any day.

Except, she had gotten through her horrendous day by thinking about being enfolded in the comfort of his arms. She had yearned for his sympathy and, instead, had gotten his short temper.

As they crossed the street, she stole a glance at him.

His swagger was in place; the only thing missing was the derisive curl of his lip. In the dim light he could have been the rebellious teenager she and the town once knew.

In the time since he had returned, he had forced her to come out of the shadows and expose all her secrets—but one, that she still loved him. Could he do the same himself, or would he resort to sarcastic defiance as he once did?

She scanned the sidewalk and frowned. A handwritten sign stuck in the grass announced that the meeting had been moved to the community room in the back.

Her step faltered; she couldn't do this alone.

Connor gripped her arm. "Would you quit dawdling? It's freezing."

"That's it." She yanked free and swung to face him. "I don't know what burr got under your skin, but you don't have to be here. I don't need you. I can face this by myself."

He swore and drew her resisting body to his. He then secured his arm around her waist, anchoring her to him. She spotted Molly Deutscher coming up the street. Nora threw her head back and glared at him. "You're making a spectacle. Release me."

"I don't think so." The tension eased from his face; amusement glinted in his eyes. He ran his bare fingers along her jaw, leaving her skin tingling. "So you can go this alone, Nora? Hmm." He placed his fingers under her chin and tilted her face. "Your eyes may be dark as the midnight sky, but they are clear as glass to me. I see all your fears."

He lowered his head and brushed her chilled lips with his. Their breaths intermingled, warmed. It was the lightest of kisses, yet tender beyond anything she had ever experienced. He leaned his forehead against hers. "I'm sorry for being distracted. It was one hell of a day, the kind only a round of boxing or a long cold beer can cure. But I'm here."

She sighed and pressed her face into his shoulder. "All you had to do was say something. I would have understood. I had a rotten day myself."

"And I want to hear about it." He kissed her temple. Miraculously the throbbing became lost in a gentle shower of pleasure. "I'm not used to sharing my problems. I'm used to being on my own." He kissed the tip of her nose, smiled and withdrew slightly.

"Come on." He laced their fingers together. "Let's go see what Doc Sims is up to."

She nodded and fell into step beside him. Inside, rows of long tables lined the room. Connor tugged her to the front section and pulled out two folding chairs. She sat and removed her jacket, folding it neatly in her lap. Connor rocked back in his chair like a kid ready for action.

A hand slapped Connor on the shoulder before Nate dropped into the chair next to them. Immediately he stretched his long legs out and crossed them at the ankle. Eve muttered crossly as she clambered over them to get to the chair next to Nora.

"Who's watching Abby?" Nora worried.

"Relax. Christina lost the coin toss. Or maybe she won since she didn't have to put up with Nate for an escort."

Nate's wink was slow. "Ah, Eve, you're breaking my heart."

"A baseball bat couldn't even make a dent."

Nora and Connor shared a glance before both broke into laughter. One more notch of tension eased inside her. She reached out and took Connor's hand. Molly rushed down the aisle and took the end chair.

Doc Sims came in with the other church elders and took his seat at a table facing the crowd. Sweeping in last to take center court was Sheila Devlin. She folded her hands on the table, her cool gaze taking in the room. She gave a small start when she saw Nora and Connor, but she didn't lose her composure.

Nora's fingers tightened on Connor's. He squeezed her hand in reassurance.

The minister took immediate control. "I don't know what my son and that woman are doing here, but this is a closed meeting."

Doc Sims shook his head. "Sheila, I invited them. And no elders meeting is ever closed, not as long as I'm serving." He cleared his throat. "You might as well hear this now. I've decided to step down from the school board."

Sheila's face paled. "This is a fine time to decide this, Irwin, when election is in a few weeks."

The doctor held up his hand. "Now, Sheila, hold on. I'm not a spring chicken anymore, and I'd like to enjoy what time I have left in more pleasurable pursuits." He gestured at David Millman and Tom Deutscher. "Just as the next generation has assumed its rightful leadership position on the church council, it's time we had fresh blood on the school board.

"And you might as well know, I'm going to support Nora. She went to the mat for Arcadia Heights on the annexation attempt by Columbus. She's got good ideas, such as fund-raiser for a new sports field at the school."

"It's too late," Sheila snapped. "The ballots have been printed."

Doc Sims shrugged. "Ballots, smallots. For years it's been the same people running unopposed. If I step down, the school board will have to consider any write-in candidate for my replacement, and I intend to recommend Nora to my fellow board members, as well."

"I won't allow it."

"It's not solely up to you."

Sheila's tone was brittle with anger. "No, but others will stand with me. An unwed mother on the school board? I don't think so."

"No, you're wrong. I support her, as does Tom." Molly stood up, pale but determined.

When Sheila glared at Tom, he swallowed so hard his Adam's apple bobbled, but he managed to nod in agreement. At the back of the room, a man called out, "I support Nora's candidacy, too."

Everyone's heads turned. Coach Krinard and his wife walked down the aisle. The pair smiled and took seats in the row behind Nora.

Nate stirred, recrossing his legs. "The Robertses stand behind Nora, as well."

"You see, Sheila?" The doctor raised his brows. "You've served our little community well, but your attitudes are a bit prehistoric for the new century."

"Are they? Then let's examine Nora's lack of judgment. She rejected David here for my good-for-nothing son."

Only the flex of Connor's fingers on Nora's revealed his true reaction. He gave a cocky grin. "Gee, thanks, Mom. Your confidence in me is humbling."

"That is so typical." Sheila rounded on him. "You've always had a smart mouth. You've never been serious a day in your life."

Connor squeezed Nora's hand before he rose and

advanced to where his mother sat. "Oh, that's where you're wrong, Pastor." He planted his palms on the table's surface. "I'm serious about my business and cultivation. I'm serious about my daughter, and I'm damn serious about her mother.

"And it will be a cold day in hell before I let you hurt either of them."

Connor looked at David, who was leaning so far back in his chair that he was in danger of toppling backward. "David, did you know that the minister once used her influence over your father to threaten Abigail McCall?"

David reared up in his chair. "What?"

"My mother has always used her position as this community's confidant to peddle favors or apply pressure. Twelve years ago, when Nora's aunt took out a loan to upgrade her studio and shop, your father was prepared to pull the financing if I didn't leave town."

The banker turned and stared at Sheila. "Pastor, is this true?"

"Your father had grave concerns about Abigail's continued financial stability."

"Put in his ear by you," Connor interjected. "You threatened to tell the bank's review board about missing funds if Mr. Millman didn't go along with your plan."

David closed his eyes briefly. When he reopened them, his gaze was calm, steady, if weary with his inner burden. "That's old news. Although it never became public knowledge, the problems with misapplication of the bank's funds were the reason Dad took an early retirement. I've since corrected the situation."

He glanced at Nora. "Rest easy that the First Community Bank of Arcadia Heights is quite happy with its recent loan to Kilning You Softly and expects to have a long and happy relationship with the shop's owners." He then addressed Connor. "And if Primal Rose should ever want to entrust a local bank with some of its finances, that owner can be assured of its safekeeping. The highest standards will be maintained on a purely business level. The days of personal feelings interfering with business ethics are gone. You have my word on it." He held out his hand.

Connor shook hands and grinned. "I'll be in touch about some expansion plans I have."

"Whether you do or not, I'll be supporting Nora's run for the school board." David folded his arms and leaned back, his participation in the confrontation clearly at an end.

Sheila pointed at Connor. "Don't think this is over. We'll see what the court thinks of you two as parents."

Doc Sims rubbed his chin. "You know, Sheila, suing your son for custody of his daughter doesn't seem to be something a church minister should do. Especially one up for promotion to a bigger ministry. Sounds like a career-ending move to me."

There was a collective gasp from the others in the room. Molly squeaked, "Doc, she's trying to take Abby?"

Sheila rose and raged at the doctor, "Are you threatening me?"

"Oh, no. I'm just giving you friendly advice, like the kind you give. I don't know why you hate your son or Nora. Don't want to know, although I think it's a real shame. However, I think your lack of charity to your own flesh and blood will weigh heavily with the general assembly."

Sheila's shoulders jerked and bowed slightly. "I'm doing it for the good of the child."

As if she had been cued to take her place on stage, Nora took a deep breath and rose. "Like you did thirty years ago, Pastor?"

Loathing filled the older woman's face. "I don't know what you're talking about."

After pulling out a fax, Nora unfolded it. "I think you do. I think you remember when you had a baby out of wedlock. Someone, your parents perhaps, altered the birth certificate to list you as a married woman with a named father."

Audible gasps filled the room, followed by the scrape of chair legs as people inched forward to hear better.

Connor looked stunned. "What?"

She walked to his side. She wanted to touch him, but his shuttered expression sent a frisson of alarm through her. "I'm sorry. I wanted to tell you first, but things didn't go as planned this evening. I've obtained a copy of your original birth certificate. Your mother's maiden name was listed and the word 'unknown' was filled in for your father's name."

Nora faced her longtime adversary. "You resent me because I'm a constant reminder of the mistake you made."

"This is not a court, and you're not my jury," Sheila advised her in chilled tones. "Unlike your mother, I've borne my penance for thirty years. And yet, it appears that the sins of the parents will live on."

She folded her hands and addressed those seated at the head table. "I've served this community for twenty-four years." She raised her hands, palms up, to the silent audience. "I've guided you, counseled you, held your hands in grief. I've earned this advancement many times over. The fact that I cannot atone for all my sins merely makes me human. Judge me as you

will. I'll not apologize nor grovel for forgiveness."
With her head held high, she left the room.

In the hush that followed, Doc Sims slowly got to
his feet. "Folks, I think this meeting is over."

Without a word, Connor turned and walked down
the aisle. No one tried to stop or speak to him. Watching the rigid set of his shoulders, Nora wondered if she
had won the battle only to lose the war.

Connor tracked down his mother exactly where he
expected to find her—standing on her pulpit. Her eyes
met his and held. And held.

"That night you threw me out of the house, you
were afraid I'd learn the truth about my illegitimacy if
I found the birth certificate." He advanced down the
aisle. "You were afraid I would expose your secret."

He climbed the short flight of steps to the platform.
"What I don't get is why you didn't simply put me up
for adoption. You weren't married. You didn't want
kids, so why did you keep me? Why bother with the
inconvenience?" He halted a few feet from the woman
who had been a mother to him biologically—but never
emotionally or spiritually.

"Penance."

If some small part of him had hoped that Sheila had
once wanted him, it was crushed forever beneath her
brutal response.

"Penance. You spent eighteen years neglecting me
in the name of penance."

"If I'd gotten rid of you, then I would have had
nothing to remind me of my fall." Her eyes glittered
coldly in the dim light. "Every time I looked at you,
I saw how far I'd fallen. Every time I looked at you, I
hated you."

His voice was raw, ragged. "Who was my father? Do you even know?"

"How dare you! I wasn't some cheap floozy like Nora's mother."

"At least Nora's mother was honest about what she was. Who was he?"

"I met him at a tent revival. When I saw him standing at the entrance, I thought our meeting was meant to be. Then I learned he was married." She stared across the empty pews as if she were seeing a different time, a different congregation. "By then it was too late. I should have known better."

"No matter how hard I tried to cut him out of you, your father kept hounding me through you."

She pointed a trembling finger at him. "You had to come back, didn't you, and ruin things for me one last time!" Her voice rose, cracked. "Haven't I paid enough for my sins?"

Connor didn't know if Sheila was talking to him or his father. He closed the distance and grabbed her shoulders. "I came back because I'd left behind someone very important to me."

"Oh, yes. That girl."

"That girl brought our daughter into the world all by herself."

"She had her family."

"She didn't have the father of her child with her."

"Well, neither did I."

He released her abruptly. Of course. It all made perverted sense. Sheila never told him about Nora's pregnancy because she wanted Nora to be alone, just as she had been.

"Retribution. That's what this has been about all along."

"Yes. You fell for a no-account who'll never know who her father is."

That reminded him. He would end at least one thing tonight. He rocked back on his heels. "Where is it?"

"What?"

"The folder you kept on the McCalls."

Her eyes flickered. He strode to the ambry and wrenched it open. Inside among the sacraments was a manila folder. He opened it and found faded, discolored newspaper clippings and letters, some on the stationery of a child-services department in northern Ohio.

"I'll take this."

"You can steal it, but you can't hide the truth about those girls."

"I can keep you from persecuting them."

"At the expense of Abby. I'll get custody."

"Not after I testify in court about how you hit me before I was old enough to hit back."

"Troublemaker versus minister? I think the scales are balanced in my favor."

"Then what about Tony?"

"Tony?"

"You don't even know the name of the kid you slugged yesterday, do you? Your days of playing minister are over, and you don't even know it."

He strode down the aisle and let the door slam on his past. He paused by the Madonna statue of Nora and Abby. His mother's hatred had stolen so much from him. Somehow he would find a way to make it up to Nora and their daughter.

After she managed to free herself from well-wishers, Nora was startled to see Connor waiting by his pickup truck. Because of his disappearing act in the church, she'd figured she'd be walking home. Without a word he went to the passenger-side door and opened it for her. She climbed in and clasped her hands together, not so much from the cold but from fear.

Grabbing the last vestiges of courage, she said, "Don't you think we should talk?"

"Not while I'm driving. Let me get you home first."

Uh-oh. Nora's heart sank.

A few minutes later he stopped in front of her house, but kept the engine running.

She kept her voice light. "You're not going to come in?"

"No, I have to get to Columbus tonight."

"What?"

"I'm flying to Florida."

She reeled. All her hopes and dreams, shattered by one simple sentence. She wanted to hide, she wanted to cry, but she summoned the one shield that had always protected her—her pride.

"I see you had your escape plan in place."

Connor swung toward her. The hard glint in his eyes, the deep grooves of anger in his face, had her backing against the cab door, fumbling for the handle. He grabbed her shoulders.

"Damn it, Nora. I'm not abandoning you. Are you ever going to trust anyone other than your sisters? Are you ever going to trust someone enough not to keep secrets?"

He swore, released her and dragged his hand through his hair. "There's a wildfire in Florida near Primal Rose's main nursery. They've had a drought for months, and some fool started a fire. My manager called me late today. I'm taking the red-eye tonight. I have to get down there to help salvage what I can before the flames reach the store."

He reached into his pocket and pulled out a set of

keys. "Here." He took her hand, dropped the keys onto her palm and pressed her fingers closed over them. "Could you please have Abby take care of Bran while I'm gone? I've already called Tony Gennaro's father and arranged for him to watch over the greenhouse and construction crews. He's on crutches, but Tony can do the heavy stuff for him after school."

His callused hands cupped her face. "I'm coming back, Nora. This is my home now. I want to watch my daughter grow into an incredibly beautiful woman. I want to keep my promise to Ed and create a botanical garden in memory of his love for his wife."

In the dim light of the dashboard, Nora watched as anguish replaced the anger in his expression.

"And I want to make a life with you, but while I'm gone, you need to ask yourself this question. Can you trust me? Because if you can't, then there's no future for us."

His dark gaze bore into her. "You know what hurt the most tonight? It wasn't finding out my mother had lied to me my entire life. It was learning that, once again, you had kept a secret from me. You had ample time to tell me, and yet you didn't."

"Connor, I—"

He broke away and jerked open the driver's door. He rounded the front of the truck and opened hers.

She tried again. "I wanted to tell you. It had just been a bad day. First Charlie telling me he couldn't handle your account anymore and then my quitting—"

"Charlie's dropping my account?"

"Your mother got to him."

This time his curse was ripe. "What am I supposed to do now? The sale of the Illinois franchise is on Thursday."

She placed a hand on his upper arm. "I'll handle it. I've got your files. I took them with me."

He studied her, a faint smile on his lips. "You really quit?"

"Yes." She started to withdraw her hand, but he enfolded it in his. "I'm thinking about setting up my own office above the pottery shop."

He kissed the back of her hand. "That's great, Nora. I'm happy for you."

Her laugh was half moan. "I'm glad you think so. I'm not so sure I haven't made a colossal mistake."

He drew her to him and stroked her cheek. "Honey, you're a much better attorney than that turkey. It was time for you to let go of that job and move on." He brushed his lips lightly over hers. She leaned into him, expecting him to deepen the kiss, but he blocked her arms and moved away.

"It's also time to let go of your fear of my leaving you. I'm going to be part of my daughter's life and I want to be a part of yours. But I need it all, Nora. I want your trust and your love." He walked to the driver's side of the truck.

She managed to call out. "That's a little one-sided."

Bracing his arm on the opened door, he shook his head. "No, it's not. Because the thing is, I love you. I always have. I want the photo album of a family." He slid in, shut the door and drove off.

She stood, staring until his taillights vanished. Finally she had the words, but not the man.

Chapter Fourteen

Friday night Nora pressed her hand in the small of her back and stretched. With a mixture of pride and trepidation, she surveyed the room above the pottery shop. The maple floor gleamed with polish; every nook and cranny was dust-free. Tomorrow after the shop closed, she and her sisters planned to repaint the walls. During a trip to the hardware store, she had managed to convince Christina that lavender might put off male clients. They eventually settled on eggshell with federal-blue accents.

From the stairwell she could hear the din of sisterly warfare emanating from the rear of the shop. Brushes clattered in a jar as Christina protested, "It was your turn to cook!"

Eve's voice was clear and firm above the sound of the back door opening. "It is. And I'm cooking Chinese takeout. We're leaving, Nora!"

"Between the two of you, a person could overdose on junk food." Then Christina yelled up the stairway, "Don't forget to turn off the lights, Nora."

Nora rolled her eyes. "Yes, Christina."

A second later the door banged, and a blessed hush crept over the room. Nora smiled and returned to unpacking a box, but the busy work wasn't enough to keep her thoughts at bay.

Connor's Florida operation was safe, and the fire was under control. She and Abby had watched the news every night, and every night before Abby's bedtime curfew, Connor had called to talk with his daughter. Although he had missed Parents' Day, he had vowed to return in time for tomorrow's soccer match.

She and Connor had limited their own conversations to business, going over the details of the franchise sale. Still, every time before he had hung up, she had waited and hoped for him to say "I love you" again. And every time had been disappointed.

I want the photo album of a family. She couldn't forget his last comment.

She had one. Because of the security of Aunt Abigail's constant unflappable love, she had memories of hot chocolate and cookies, of childish pictures hung on the refrigerator door, of bedtime stories about magical places and of arms holding her when she woke up screaming from a nightmare.

Nora sat back on her heels and considered her new life. She was not only running for the school board but was also starting her own law firm. She could hug herself with sheer wonderment.

Her life was no longer wrapped in responsibilities for everyone but herself. At last she could embrace her own future. All she had to do was take one more chance, a chance on Connor. She could give him his own pictures of love.

From the box before her she lifted a small framed photograph and studied the image. Yes, this was perfect. She grabbed a few sheets of the white tissue paper and carefully rewrapped the photo.

She rose and slid the bundle into her outdoor jacket. Hooking the jacket over her arm, she crossed to the door. Her hand on the light switch, she paused and scanned the room once more.

Mine, she thought fiercely. This will be my own practice. She flicked off the switch and went downstairs. Since it was already a ritual among the sisters to turn off the spotlight on the *Sisters Three* statue as the last closing act, she entered the main room of the shop. She halted, surprised by the scene that met her eyes.

At a table by the fireplace sat Abby and Connor, bent in concentration over a painted figurine. Her heart melted at the sight of daughter and father together, so completely in tune with each other. Behind them, the *Sisters Three* glowed.

Nora's eyes watered. How she wanted to hold on to this moment forever.

"You need more black there, Dad." Abby gestured with her brush.

Nora followed the pointing tip and looked at the figurine. The body was orange with black stripes, its eyes black slits, its mouth smugly curved.

She recognized it immediately; it was the mother cat from the farm. She draped her coat over a chair and said, "Hi, you two. Is this a private party or can I join you?"

Two startled pairs of identical blue eyes looked up,

then at each other in guilty alarm. Abby frowned. "Mom, you're too early. We're not ready yet."

Nora strolled over and planted a light kiss on her daughter's forehead. "Yes, dear, I had a very nice day. And how was yours?"

Abby stuck out her tongue. "Oh, Mom." She brushed the wisps of hair off her cheek.

Nora put her arm around her child's shoulders and nodded to the man whose gaze was searing her. "You're back," she said, then immediately blushed. Talk about the obvious.

His mouth kicked up at the corners. "Good evening, Nora."

She regarded the object on the table. Although the colors seemed garish now, she knew from experience that when the figurine had been glazed and fired, it would be striking. Her daughter had Abigail's and Christina's artistic flair, no doubt about it.

"It's supposed to be a surprise for you. A replacement for the broken one," Abby explained.

"Not a replacement," Nora murmured, brushed her lips across her daughter's forehead again. "A new keepsake to cherish."

"You like it?"

"I love it."

"Let's put it by the kiln for Christina to finish up later," Connor suggested, rising as he spoke, "and get you home for dinner. Your mother and I are going to take a walk." He winked.

To Nora's amazement, Abby cradled the figurine and headed straight to the rear room. Her daughter didn't dawdle as they crossed the yard to the house, although she did talk a mile a minute about her upcoming game.

Only when she stood on the porch stoop did Abby linger, starring at her sneakers. "Uh, Dad?"

A little tingle raced along Nora's spine. Her child had a father in her life, something she herself had never had.

"Yes, hon?" Connor braced his foot on the lower step.

Abby smiled. "Thanks for making it back in time for my game."

"I'll be rooting for you tomorrow and eating one too many hot dogs."

Their eyes met and held. Then, like a cannonball, Abby launched herself at Connor and hugged him. "I'll score a point just for you."

Nora pressed a palm to her chest, hoping to keep her heart from exploding with joy. She managed to ask lightly, "And what about me?"

Abby released Connor and gave her a quick but super-size squeeze. ":Sure, Mom. I'll score a point for you." She whispered conspiratorially, "You have fun. Don't hurry home on my account."

"Scoot."

Nora looked at Connor, only to have her pulse pick up a notch. With his bomber-jacket collar up, chill-flushed cheeks and wind-ruffled hair, he was gloriously male. He offered his hand. "Come with me?"

Find the magic, Nora.

She blinked. Was that her aunt's voice quivering on the night air, or was it merely her soul whispering to her?

Didn't matter. She was ready. She held out her hand to meet his.

Connor guided her across the lawn once more and

then into the woods. From his jacket pocket, he pulled out a pair of small flashlights and gave her one.

The raw wind didn't penetrate the inner sanctum of the forest. Above, the treetops sighed like lovers. Below, the woods' residents crept about their nocturnal activities with just a whisper of sound.

Nora kept her flashlight aimed so that its circle of light illuminated the path in front of them. The world beyond the beam remained inviolate.

With each step, she walked past her nightmares, fears and heartbreaks; each step brought her closer to her dreams, hopes and expectations.

When the trail narrowed, Connor's hand released hers and fell to her waist, tucking Nora unresistingly into the warmth of his body. As if they had been split asunder from the same mold, their bodies now melded together, her softness perfectly matching his hard planes.

Then she drew in a sharp breath, for Connor's strong fingers had spanned across the yielding area of her stomach. Despite her protective layers of clothing, his searing touch sent heat all the way to her core. A longing slowly unfurled inside her, tendrils of yearning so much deeper than she had ever experienced. Connor's fingers flexed, digging into her flesh. Anticipation flared, raked her insides.

They reached the other side of the forest. Instead of taking the path to the right, toward the farmhouse, Connor veered left. A minute later the trail split. The wider branch broke into the open expanse of land near the lake; the smaller one led to a secluded alcove by the water. Connor took the latter.

He was taking her to their place.

Silvery light from the half moon dappled the clearing. Nora switched off her flashlight, and Connor followed suit. Even as she stepped into it, she felt the familiar sense of freedom, the lifting of all her worries and responsibilities. Sheltered from prying eyes but open to the vista of the lake, the spot had been her favorite since she had begun exploring the woods.

The very first time she had stumbled across the spot, she had cried over the death of her mother and the loss of her childish dream—one in which her mother had loved her. After that, she had come to the clearing to ponder her growing feelings for the aunt who had taken in her sisters and her.

Sometimes she had come to the spot because she wanted the tranquillity that came from watching the lake on a hot summer day. The spot was where she had first seen Connor Devlin's flashing smile. His fierce concentration, even when engaged in boyish activities, had enthralled her.

Years later she had allowed the boy to become her lover. And he had given her the most precious living memory of that first love—Abby.

Nora stopped in the middle of the clearing. Connor knelt beside a circle of stones. "I laid a fire before coming over. There's blankets by the oak and a picnic supper in the basket."

"Sounds like you thought of everything."

He struck a match. "I did pack a better menu than what we had as kids."

"I don't know," Nora said as she watched the kindling flare, "I rather liked the sodas and marshmallows."

He stuck his hands in his pockets. Nora realized he didn't know what to do next. For some reason his discomfort thrilled her. The moment was hers.

"Connor?"

"Yes?" He looked over.

Time to pull an "Abby." Nora raced across the clearing and threw her arms around him. "Welcome home."

His heart hammering wildly, Connor enfolded Nora in his arms and pressed his cheek against the crown of her head.

He could smell her scent, the hint of femininity that always clung to her. Woman. That was the scent of Nora.

Reaching the rim of her turtleneck, he tugged it down and pressed his lips to the warm skin at the base of her throat. His reward was the jolt of her pulse; his penance was the hot need slamming into him like a velvet fist. Connor stood at the edge of a dark vortex of hunger and struggled to rein in his control.

He raised his head. "If you're hungry, there're marshmallows to roast."

"Ah, my hero. Moonlight and marshmallows." Nora's laugh was sensual, more intoxicating than any glass of champagne. It slipped into his blood and sizzled. She tightened her hold on him and kissed his jaw—a rose-petal kiss, soft, sweet and sumptuous. "I missed you." Her scent, mingled with moondust, seduced his system.

He tumbled into passion's storm.

Nora was in his arms, and he would never let her go again. He belonged with her. His mind accepted what his heart had known all along.

Urgently he lowered her to the carefully arranged blankets. His tongue outlined the tender curves of her mouth, demanding an invitation. Her lips parted in compliance, and he delved into her lush warmth, taking it, plundering it.

Nora's arms crept around his neck, her fingers brushed, dug, into the waves of his hair. The sensation fired up his blood another notch. Desperate to touch more of her, he found the zipper to her jacket and lowered it. Her hands joined his in tugging the hem of her turtleneck from the waistband of her pants.

His fingers skimmed along her sides. She inhaled deeply beneath him and arched into his touch. With a quick movement he unfastened her bra and cupped her breasts. He paused to let his racing senses simmer, to savor the essence of the woman.

Her torso was elegant, long and slender. In the moonlight her satiny skin was transformed into the creamy white of a Crystalline rose. Her breasts were high and firm, filling his hands. At their centers, dark buds puckered expectantly. Gently he skimmed the rough pad of his thumb over her nipple and grinned with triumph when she twisted beneath him. Lowering his head, he sampled the smooth curve of one breast. Then, unable to deny himself any longer, he suckled.

He struggled to stop his desperate rush to completion, to bring her pleasure first. He had waited for what seemed like an eternity this past week, and he thought he could delay his taking for as long as necessary. What he hadn't anticipated was the pure female passion coming alive, burning him with its heat.

Nora reared up and snaked her hands under his jacket. She tore open his shirt and raced her hands over his chest, digging her fingers into the hair. Desire stabbed Connor, but he tried to stop her tormenting fingers. ''Nora, honey, slow down.''

Ignoring him, she fumbled with the button on his

jeans. Before he could stop her, she had his zipper down. Hot needy hands shot across his torso and encircled him. Connor's best-laid plans went down with his pants. He jerked Nora's pants open and dragged them over her arching hips. His fingers found her wet heat and all reason fled his mind. He rolled between her thighs, keeping his weight on his arms. Nora wrapped her legs around his waist.

He swooped down and captured her mouth, plundering it, as he slid into her heat. One last remnant of his mind registered how perfectly she fit him, and then her hips lunged against his. He withdrew slightly and plunged to the depth of her core. Together they found a timeless rhythm. Then Nora let go in his arms, and Connor found himself swept along with her.

Though Nora's eyes were closed, she could feel every inch of his heated flesh, every crisp tickling hair on his body. She lay tucked against Connor within the protective circle of his arms—strong arms roped with lean work-hardened muscles. He shifted, the movement brushing his semi-aroused manhood against her.

"Are you okay?" His husky voice rippled through her very soul. Her eyes slowly opened. Connor was watching her, his hooded gaze satisfied. He reached out and skimmed his knuckles along her jaw.

"I'm fine." She turned her head and kissed the back of his hand. Her stomach rumbled, and his hand lowered, caressed her belly. A different kind of hunger flared, but with a laugh Connor rose and tucked the blanket around her.

"I guess I'd better feed you."

"Marshmallows are such an important food group for picnics."

"Smart aleck. See if I share my brie, crackers and grapes with you now."

"Mmm, sounds good." She propped herself on her elbow to enjoy the view.

His bronze muscular body was a thing of beauty in the flickering firelight. "Abigail would have loved to have sculpted you."

He flashed a startled glance at her as he knelt before the basket. "Me?"

"A living breathing form of pure masculinity? You bet."

A dark flush crept across his cheeks. She wanted to press her lips against that heated flesh. Lust was addictive, she realized, maybe too addictive. Was this what her mother had experienced, an insatiable need?

No, she was not her mother; she couldn't be. She only felt this aching need with Connor. No other man moved her as he did, made her feel this way. His hands made her fly.

Shaking off her dark thoughts, she sat up, grabbed the blanket by her feet and wrapped herself in it as she rose. She crossed to the log and sat facing the fire. Connor carried the basket over, set it on the ground and crouched beside it. A white china plate clinked as he brought it out. He laid out other wrapped packages. With rapid movements he pulled out a Swiss Army knife, opened one of the packages, sliced through a wedge of cheese. He unwrapped another and added grapes to the plate. He handed the offering to her, which she accepted with a murmured thank-you.

Connor next pulled out a long-necked bottle of champagne. He removed the foil and protective wire holder and popped the cork. He reached into the basket and removed a flute. The liquid hissed as he filled the glass. After replacing the bottle in the basket, he stood with a white rose in his other hand. His smile was positively wicked.

Hot memories of another rose flowed through her. "Oh, no. No, you don't. Not until we've eaten." Laughing, Nora balanced her plate in one hand and opened the blanket.

"For later, then." He set the rose on top of the basket and sat next to her so his cool hip pressed against hers. He wrapped the blanket around them, creating a cozy cocoon.

"Here." Instead of more food, Connor handed her a folder.

"What's this?" She flipped it open and squinted in the flickering light.

"Mom's folder on you and your sisters."

Despite the fire, the blanket and Connor's warmth, Nora felt cold slash to her bones. She carefully set her plate on the ground. Her fingers trembled as she sorted through the documents: newspaper clippings about her mother's death, letters and case summaries from child-support services, an investigator's report. Rage chased the chill from her. "She snooped on us?"

"It looks that way."

"Where did you get this?"

"I found it in the pulpit area the night of the elders' meeting."

"You've had this since Monday night and you're just now showing it to me?" She tried to surge to her feet, but he hooked his arm around her waist and kept her anchored next to him.

"Hey, I had a flight to catch that night. I didn't know what was in the folder until I could look through it on the plane."

The tension began to ease from her.

"I didn't think I should tell you about it on the phone. There have been times I could swear everyone in Arcadia has switchboard access to all the phone lines."

She relaxed against him, absorbing his warmth, hoping it would melt the last few icicles of fear deep inside her.

"It will be up to you and your sisters whether anything in there should be used in the custody dispute."

"Oh, I didn't get a chance to tell you." She twisted to look into his face. "The judge heard our motion to dismiss the petition and granted it."

His hand tightened on her waist. "Translate the lawyer-speak. Does that mean it's over?"

She shook her head. "Your mother could have filed again, but Brad told me that Sheila has instructed her attorney to drop the suit."

"So it's over."

Nora looked at the papers in her lap. "Not quite. Did you read—"

"No." Connor stroked her face. "No, honey, I didn't. I figured we had a lifetime together for you to tell me about your past, if you want to."

She covered his hand with hers. "I want to, Connor." She leaned forward and kissed him softly, a promise to be kept. She then drew away, leaned forward and fed a page of the report about her to the fire. "I'll show Christina and Eve the papers that concern them and let them decide what they want to do, but as for me…"

Connor indicated the fire. "Have at it, honey."

She did. There was one page for the times her mother left them alone.

One for the hunger.

One for the closet and the monsters who lurked there.

One for the father she'd never had.

One for the mother who had died without saying words of love.

As each piece of paper twisted, blackened and disappeared into the heart of the fire, she felt her fears fade away. Peace eased into their place. When she had finished, she laid the folder on the ground. "How about a glass of—"

She broke off in a gasp as Connor lifted and settled her on his lap. "Wrap the blanket behind me," he instructed.

She did so, gliding her hands along his muscular upper back. He tucked the cover around them both. Lured by the heat of his body, Nora allowed her head to rest in the musky hollow between his neck and shoulder. Slowly he slid his hand up and down her arm, leaving a wake of oversensitized nerve endings in its path.

She gazed dreamily at the dancing flames. Tonight was everything she had hoped for and more. She could never have imagined such a feeling of contentedness, of wholeness.

"When we were young, my sisters and I used to play make-believe about our fathers. They were princes, movies stars, wealthy playboys who, if they knew of our existence, would come back into our lives and sweep us away to golden castles, to live happily ever after."

Connor kissed her temple, the tenderness of the caress nearly her undoing. She swallowed. "I never believed in the fantasies we spun. It was just a game to keep Christina and Eve occupied during the long nights when our mother was off with who knew what guy." She had seen the men her mother had brought home. She knew the truth about what kind of men their fathers were.

"I didn't know what love was until we went to live with Abigail."

His arms tightened around her. "Your aunt was special."

"You don't know how special."

He traced his finger down her cheek and then pulled it away. On its tip she could see her tear glistening.

"If your aunt were here, she would have been rolling up her sleeves, anxious to capture this moment, to sculpt your love for her." He slowly lowered his hand and closed his fingers over the tear. "Much like she did with the *Madonna.*"

"No, you're wrong." She searched for her jacket and found it off to the side of the blanket. "She would be capturing this moment with you." She slipped her hand into the jacket pocket and pulled out the bundled package. "She told me to find the magic in life." After removing the tissue, she gave him the small photograph of her holding Abby as a baby—the basis of her aunt's statue.

"I've found the magic, Connor. With you. I love you. I want to be a family with you and Abby."

Connor had never believed mere words could move the earth.

How wrong he had been. Three words from the right person could change a life. All his dreams of a family, of permanent roots, were here now, within his grasp.

"I love you." He gazed into her wonderful eyes and saw his future mirrored in their crystal depths.

He continued, "I never stopped loving you, but I kept a snapshot in my mind of you as an adoring eighteen-year-old who thought I could do no wrong. That outdated memory didn't do justice to the woman you've become. I love you for having my child. I love your pride and courage. I love you, Nora."

He feathered kisses, gentle and soft, over her face. Her mouth sought his, captured his lips in a sumptuous kiss. Her body was molten, warm and pliant, sending licks of desire through his system.

She pressed herself against his chest and deepened the kiss. At her sweet response a shattering revelation struck him. For the past week he had tried to bind Nora to him. Somewhere along the way, he had bound himself to her.

Forever.

"Connor—" Nora gave a delightful wiggle on his lap "—what about the rose?"

"We'll save it." Though the idea gave him pause. He gathered her and lowered her to the quilt. "This time I want to make love to you so slowly and thoroughly you'll scream the treetops off."

He stretched out beside her. He lifted the blanket and inhaled sharply. Her smooth skin glowed in the firelight, beckoning his touch.

He caressed each ridge, every indentation of her rib cage, smiling at her sharp intake of breath. He slid his hand upward until he cupped her breast. Savoring the weight of it, he skimmed his thumb over its bud until it flowered beneath his touch.

When Nora tried to lift her hips and curl her legs around him, he covered her. "No, honey. It seems every time we've made love, it's been all raging fire. This time, let me show you the simple pleasures of desire.''

He nudged away her hair and planted light kisses along her neck. She sighed, her body becoming liquid beneath his touch. Connor smiled and let his hands stroke, explore and cherish every inch of her skin.

This time he let his body hear hers. Every throaty moan, every delicate shudder, every vibrating need.

And when his fingers caressed her moist softness until she cried out, only then did he slide into her. A murmured sigh was released as they moved together. Hers? His? He didn't know. He only knew that as he swept over the peak with her, her name tumbled from his lips.

Arcadia Heights was firmly in the cold grip of November. Not even the humid heat of his nursery could chase away the chill that had invaded Connor during his brief trip from the house to the nursery. He frowned and studied his handiwork. He then picked up his pruning shears and clipped one more time. There, perfect.

He picked up his prize and walked outside. The chill wind buffeted him, but he stopped halfway to the farmhouse and slowly turned. A white blanket of snow covered the gentle swells of the hills. Even the dark sentinels of trees wore their holiday glitter of ice.

Gone were the dilapidated sheds that once stood there. In their place were new buildings. The greenhouse, its glass walls frosted, glowed translucently against the landscape.

This was all his. His home.

Two weeks ago his mother had left town for her new post. She hadn't gotten the parish she'd wanted. Instead, the church had transferred her to an administrative position. In a brief bitter phone call, she had blamed him for her lost promotion and had made it clear she never wanted to see him again. While Connor had suffered a sense of loss for the love he'd never had from his mother, he had known that her departure was for the best. Whatever pall she might have cast over his happiness with Nora and Abby was gone.

He turned back to the house. The McCall sisters and Nate Roberts were coming for Thanksgiving dinner. No time to stand around daydreaming. He climbed to the landing and stomped the snow off his boots.

Smiling, he opened the kitchen door. Inside, the blue-and-white-tile floor glistened, rich wood cabinets with brass fittings glowed, and the blue counters sparkled. Sheer curtains let in the dawn's early glow. The odor of overbrewed coffee mingled with the smoky scent of frying bacon. At the glossy white stove stood Nora, her long black hair pulled carelessly into a ponytail.

Instead of smiling and blowing him a kiss, she glared over her shoulder. "You're back too soon. You're ruining my surprise."

Hiding his hand behind his back, Connor crossed to her and kissed the tip of her nose. He reached around her and turned off the burners. "Smells like it's already ruined." He set the pan of blackened bacon aside.

She dropped the tongs onto the stovetop with a clatter. "It was just fine a minute ago. I don't understand what happened."

Connor smiled as he drew her close. "I don't, either, sweetheart. But—" he kissed her brow "—it's the thought that counts."

Nora nuzzled his neck. "I wanted to give you your

fantasy. Abby told me you had this vision of me cooking breakfast in the kitchen.''

He brushed another kiss across her brow, seeking to smooth the furrows there. ''And a lovely fantasy you've brought me.''

She waved a hand at the stove. ''But it's spoiled. And we have guests coming for dinner.''

He ran his thumb along the graceful line of her cheek. ''We can always call Eve and ask her to bring takeout Chinese.''

Nora's mouth curved. ''We could at that.''

''But first—'' Connor brought his other hand around ''—here's a rose for you.'' The blossom was a dove-gray, as soft as the expression in Nora's eyes.

''Connor, it's beautiful.'' She ran a finger along the petal, exposing its white underside. ''I've never seen anything so exquisite.''

His heart hammering, Connor managed to say, ''That's because I cultivated the new hybrid tea for you. I'll be presenting Nora's Pride at the Rose Hybridizers Association in the spring.''

Nora's smile bloomed. ''You named it after me?''

He cupped her chin. ''Sweetheart, I created it for you and you alone.'' He lowered his head and kissed her mouth. When she sought to deepen the kiss, he drew back slightly. ''You haven't checked out the bow.''

''Oh.'' Nora's gaze dropped to the red bow. ''Very pretty…'' Her voice trailed off. The flower petals trembled.

Carefully he plucked the rose from her hand and untied the satin. Nestled in the loop was an engagement ring, a luminous black pearl encircled by tiny diamonds. Taking her hand, he slid the ring on her finger and whispered, ''Will you marry me, Nora McCall?''

Her eyes, more beautiful than any flower could ever be, glittered with love and amusement. "I guess I'd better say yes."

Puzzled, Connor arched a brow.

Nora drew his face close to hers. "Because this time we're going to have a baby together."

Connor wrapped her in his arms and poured all his love into the kiss. He had a house, a daughter, a baby on the way and the woman he loved. He finally had his home.

* * * * *

Silhouette presents an exciting new continuity series:

CROWN AND GLORY

When a royal family rolls out the red carpet for love, power and deception, will their lives change forever?

The saga begins in April 2002 with:

The Princess Is Pregnant!

by Laurie Paige (SE #1459)

May: THE PRINCESS AND THE DUKE by Allison Leigh
(SE #1465)

June: ROYAL PROTOCOL by Christine Flynn
(SE #1471)

Be sure to catch all nine Crown and Glory stories: the first three appear in Silhouette Special Edition, the next three continue in Silhouette Romance and the saga concludes with three books in Silhouette Desire.

———————————————

And be sure not to miss more royal stories,
from Silhouette Intimate Moments'

Romancing the Crown,

running January through December.

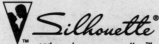

Silhouette ®
Where love comes alive ™

Available at your favorite retail outlet.

Visit Silhouette at www.eHarlequin.com

SSECAG

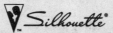

Where Texas society reigns supreme—and appearances are everything.

Coming in June 2002
Stroke of Fortune by Christine Rimmer

Millionaire rancher and eligible bachelor Flynt Carson struck a hole in one when his Sunday golf ritual at the Lone Star Country Club unveiled an abandoned baby girl. Flynt felt he had no business raising a child, and desperately needed the help of former flame Josie Lavender. Though this woman was too innocent for his tarnished soul, the love-struck nanny was determined to help him raise the mysterious baby—and what happened next was anyone's guess!

Available at your favorite retail outlet.

Where love comes alive™

Visit Silhouette at www.eHarlequin.com

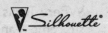